George L. Raymond

Columbus the Discoverer

A drama

George L. Raymond

Columbus the Discoverer
A drama

ISBN/EAN: 9783337344207

Printed in Europe, USA, Canada, Australia, Japan

Cover: Foto ©Andreas Hilbeck / pixelio.de

More available books at **www.hansebooks.com**

COLUMBUS THE DISCOVERER

A DRAMA

BY
WALTER WARREN

BOSTON
ARENA PUBLISHING COMPANY
COPLEY SQUARE
1893

Arena Press.

THE FOLLOWING CHARACTERS APPEAR ONLY IN THE FOLLOWING ACTS.

In the First Act Only.

James of Mallorca,
Correo,
Tailor,
Grocer,

Waiter,
Felipa,
Dona Correo,
Woman.

In the Second Act Only.

Fernandez,
Talavera,
St. Angel,

Zalora,
Perez,
Other Monk.

Attendant.

Only after the First, in the Second and later Acts.

King Ferdinand,
Gutierrez,
Sanchez,

Arana,
Beatrix,
Queen Isabella,

Mendoza.

Only after the Second and in later Acts.

Escobar,   Pintor,   Roldan.

Only in the Fifth Act.

Velasquez,
Gamez,

Young Diego,
Fernando,

Indian.

CHARACTERS.

Columbus (Christopher)....The Discoverer of America.
Diego (Columbus)........ } Brothers of Christopher Colum-
Bartholomew (Columbus). } bus.
Fonseca .... Archdeacon of Seville, Traveler in
                          Portugal, afterwards Bishop of
                          Badajos, Palentia and Burgos;
                          then Patriarch of the Indies.
Breviesca................. A Portuguese, friend of Fonseca,
                          then later his Secretary, Treas-
                          urer and Agent in Spain.
King Ferdinand.......... Of Arragon, and, after Marriage,
                          of Spain.
Gutierrez................ Gentleman of the Spanish King's
                          Bedchamber, and Officer.
Sanchez................... Officer, Inspector-General of Co-
                          lumbus' Expedition.
James of Mellora........ President of the Portuguese Naval
                          School.
Correo................... Husband of Sister of Felipa, Co-
                          lumbus' Wife.
Fernandez................ Physician and Scientist of Spain.
Mendoza .... Archbishop of Toledo, Grand Car-
                          dinal of Spain.
Talavera................. Bishop of Avila, Confessor to the
                          Queen.
St. Angel .... Receiver of Ecclesiastical Rev-
                          enues of Aragon.
Zalora................... } Bishops of Spain.
Arana................... }
Perez .... A Monk, subsequently Prior of
                          the Convent of La Rabida near
                          Palos.

Escobar.................. ⎫
Pintor.................. ⎬ Sailors with Columbus, Settlers
Roldan................. ⎭ in the New World.
Velasquez.................Subtreasurer in Hispaniola.
Gamez...................A young Spanish nobleman, Set-
                           tler in the New World.
Young Diego.............Eldest Son of Columbus.
Fernando................Youngest son of Columbus.
Tailor.................. ⎰
Grocer.................. ⎱ In the First Act.
Waiter.................. ⎭
Moor................... ⎱
Other Monk.............. ⎰ In the Second Act.
Attendant............... ⎭
Indian..................In the Fifth Act.
Felipa..................Wife of Columbus, Mother of
                           young Diego.
Beatrix.................Companion of Columbus after
                           Felipa's death, Mother of Fer-
                           nando Columbus.
Queen Isabella..........Of Castile and, after Marriage, of
                           Spain.
Dona Correo.............Sister of Felipa, wife of Correo.
Woman..................In the First Act.
Maid...................In First and other Acts.

Citizens, Officers, Soldiers, Courtiers, Sailors, Settlers,
Women, etc.

COLUMBUS THE DISCOVERER.

ARGUMENT.

This drama is intended to be a study, psychologic rather than historic, though not unhistoric, of the character of Columbus, as manifested and developed in connection with his experiences before, during and after his discovery of America. The general outline of the plot is as follows:

ACT FIRST: *In Portugal*. SCENE FIRST: A public square. Talk about the plans of Columbus and about himself. His entrance, his introduction to Felipa, and invitation to her house. SCENE SECOND: Room in the house of Felipa. Reasons why Columbus hopes for success, the failure of his hopes, and his betrothal. SCENE THIRD: Same room ten years later, rearranged as study of Columbus. Hounded by his creditors and wronged by the King, he loses Felipa by death and decides to leave Portugal.

ACT SECOND: *In Spain*. SCENE FIRST: A Spanish camp at midnight. Columbus has enlisted

as a soldier, is ridiculed for his schemes, has a talk
with Beatrix, is present at an attempted assassina-
tion of the Queen, and thus comes to meet the
King.   SCENE SECOND: The Council of Salamanca,
called to confer with Columbus and discuss his
projects.   A summary of the popular objections
urged against them.   SCENE THIRD: The exterior of
the convent of La Rabida.   To prevent Columbus
from leaving her country, and to insure the sucess of
his plans, the Queen pledges to him the Crown jewels
of Castile.

ACT THIRD: *In Transit.*   SCENE FIRST: A street
in Palos near its harbor.   The difficulties and opposition encountered by Columbus when preparing to
sail, coming from his friends, as Beatrix, and from
his enemies, who try even to destroy his boats.   SCENE
SECOND: The deck of his ship at sea.   The muti-
neers, their talk when alone and when with Columbus, and his dealing with it.   The midnight discovery
of land, and the morning approach to it.

ACT FOURTH: *In Triumph.*   SCENE FIRST:
Room in a house at Palos.   Columbus welcomed
by Beatrix, and urged to secure benefits from the
Crown; and his description to her and to Diego of his
voyage and the new land.   SCENE SECOND: Reception at the palace of Barcelona by the King, Queen
and populace.   SCENE THIRD: Dining hall in the
house of Cardinal Mendoza.   The egg story.

ACT FIFTH: *In Chains.*   SCENE FIRST: Camp in

Hispaniola. Opposition to Columbus on the part
of noblemen and imported criminals. Placed in
chains by his enemies. SCENE SECOND: House in
Seville. Death of Columbus. SCENE THIRD: A
final tableau with hymn, representing a vision of
Columbus, when dying, of the progress and present
condition of America.

ACT FIRST.

SCENE FIRST.—*A street or square in Lisbon, Portugal. Backing at the right, a Wineshop, in front of which are two tables each with four chairs about it. Backing at the left, a convent wall ending against a chapel, the door of which faces the audience. At the sides to right and left, are houses and trees. Entrances at the Right Center through the door of the wineshop ; at the Left Center through a curtain hanging in the doorway of chapel ; and at the Right and Left Sides through streets. The curtain rising discloses* FONSECA *and* JAMES OF MALLORCA *seated at the table to the extreme Right. As the scene opens, the following is chanted by an unseen choir in the chapel.*

> O Life divine, thou art the spring
>   Of all that germs and grows,
> The Light behind the suns that bring
>   The harvests to their close.
>
> O Life divine, thou art the source,
>   Of truth within the soul ;
> Thou art the guide through all the course
>   That leads it to its goal.
>
> O Life divine, what soul succeeds
>   In aught on earth but he
> Who moves as all desires and deeds
>   Are lured and led by thee !

*Enter—Left Side—*BREVIESCA, *and sits at the table to the Left.*

FONSECA (*to* JAMES). And you came here?

JAMES. To see Columbus.

FONSECA. Him?
A crank,—what's worse, a creaking crank!

JAMES. Without
Some crank to creak of it, men might forget
The wheels of thought were made to move them
    on.

FONSECA. You start thought on the right track
    once, you'll find
What moves it on is not what moves it off.
They differ.

BREVIESCA (*to himself*). Yes, I'll wait till church is
    out:
We'll meet by accident. I'll home with her,
And fish an invitation to her house—
A lovely girl, Felipa!—As I live—

*Enter—Left Side—*DIEGO.

That man I met when traveling in Spain!
He's always looming up. I wonder what
Should bring him here to Lisbon?

DIEGO (*to* BREVIESCA). Why—this you?

BREVIESCA. Good-day, Diego.

DIEGO (*looking toward the chapel*). Same to you—
    I see—
At your devotions that you told me of—
Front door ones, too!—No wonder you deemed
    strange

My studying for the priesthood!

BREVIESCA. But you said
That you had turned from it.

DIEGO. Oh yes! Truth is
That I'm in love too,—but I love myself.

BREVIESCA. You're candid.

DIEGO. Wish to be. That's why I changed.
God started man; man's deviltry the priest.
For me, I like the thing God started best.

BREVIESCA. Like others, eh?—yet like yourself.

DIEGO. I do;
That is, we two do—God and I.

BREVIESCA. And now
They style you, " Your Irreverence "?

DIEGO. I'm reverent.

BREVIESCA. A different point of view!

DIEGO. That's all. Ay, ay;
Your soul-side down. 'tis one; if up. the other.

FONSECA (to BREVIESCA, *rising and going toward him
with* JAMES). Breviesca, as I think.

BREVIESCA (to FONSECA). Your thought is right.

FONSECA. My name's Fonseca—Spaniard – met you
once
In Seville. You recall?—

BREVIESCA (*rising*). Archdeacon—yes.
You honor me.

FONSECA. You pleased me when we met.
(*Introducing* JAMES.)
James of Mallorca, of the naval school.

BREVIESCA (*introducing* DIEGO).

   And Don Diego of——(*hesitating*).

DIEGO.   The world.

BREVIESCA.   Quite true!

DIEGO. A traveler, knowing little—would know
     more.

JAMES. If so, a man to my own heart. We thought
     You might have seen Columbus here?

*Enter—Left Center—*FELIPA, CORREO *and* DONA
         CORREO.

BREVIESCA.   No. (*Then seeing* FELIPA.) Ah!

DIEGO (*to* JAMES, *as he looks at* FELIPA).

   A pretty point, too, for his exclamation.

JAMES (*to* DIEGO. Would you see more of it?
  (*To* FELIPA.)   Good-day.

FELIPA *and* DONA CORREO.   Good-day.

CORREO (*to all*). Good-day.

JAMES (*introducing* DIEGO).

        The Don Diego, like ourselves,
  A traveler (*introducing the three to* DIEGO).

            The Dona Correo,
Felipa and Don Correo—You'll sit, not so?
And, waiter—

     *Enter—Right Center—*WAITER.
           Wine here.

WAITER.   Red or white?

JAMES (*to all*). What say you?

DONA C.   None for me, thanks.

JAMES (*to* FELIPA).　　　　　You?

FELIPA.　　　　　　　　　　Nor me.

JAMES (*to the others*).　The gentlemen, at least?

CORREO.　　　　　　　　I don't know but——

JAMES.　I thought it.　(*to other gentlemen.*)　You
　　too?—White, not so?　Its hue
　Will fit this sunny air, and make us think
　We're drinking in the sunshine!
　　　　　(*Pays the waiter for the wine.*)

　　　　　　　　[*Exit—Right Center—*WAITER.

　　　(*All seat themselves at the tables, from left to
　　　right, in this order: first empty chair,
　　　then* DIEGO, D. CORREO, CORREO, FELIPA,
　　　JAMES, BREVIESCA *and* FONSECA.　JAMES
　　　continues to* CORREO.)
　　　　　　　　　　　Did you see
　Columbus in the church?

CORREO.　　　　　　Don't know him.

JAMES.　　　　　　　　　　No?—
　A sailor, drawing maps now for our school—

FONSECA.　Who should be kept to that and facts—
　　not draw
　So much upon his fancy.

JAMES.　　　　　　　You should hear
　His arguments.

FONSECA.　　　　Say feel them—all their points
　Dipped deep in pagan poison.

JAMES.　　　　　　　　Oh, not all!

FONSECA.   Enough to make all deadly.

JAMES.   I've no scent
To follow up the trail of your dislike.

FONSECA.   You know a priest should save the world
      from lies?

JAMES.   I'm just as senseless.

          *Enter—Right Center—*WAITER *with five glasses
            of wine, and sets them before the gentlemen.*

FONSECA.   Put it this way then :
If what he says be right, the church is wrong.

JAMES.   Oh, not so bad as that !—has not found out.

FONSECA.   If what he says be wrong, his dupes will
      drown.   (*to* CORREO.)
Not so?

CORREO.   Beg pardon. 'Tis the first time yet
      I've heard of him.

FONSECA.   You'll do it soon enough.
The surest proof we men are not all fools,
Is in the way we brute them when we find them.

DIEGO.   Ay, and the surest proof we're not all
      brutes,

          *Exit—Right Center—*WAITER.

Is in the way our thinkers make us mind them.

JAMES.   So, you're his friend, eh ?

DIEGO.   Yes.

CORREO.   Have known him long ?—
Can tell us of him ?

DIEGO.   He's a Genoese.
A mathematician, studied at Pavía.

Since then, till now, for more than twenty years,
A sailor and a soldier—in the scrubs
At Naples, Tunis, famous for his fights
Against the infidel—last year, the man
Who clampt his smaller bark against a huge
Venetian galley, and when both took fire,
Forced to the waters, holding but an oar,
Swam in to Lisbon ; and that oar of his,
All that he brought here, may yet prove to be
The scepter-symbol of the mightiest sway
Your sovereign ever dreamed of.

CORREO.   Ah !—How so ?

FELIPA.   Yes, yes !

DIEGO.   His plan is now to sail around
The world ; and in the trail that's left behind
Loop all to Portugal.

FELIPA.   Around the world ?

JAMES.   Oh, you should hear him talk !

FONSECA.   No, no, should not—
A mad dog to be muzzled !

DIEGO (*to* FELIPA).   You should not—
Unless you wish to think and feel, and thrill
To feel, that there's a larger world than this.

BREVIESCA.   In one's imagination.

DIEGO.   Be it so,
Imagination is the soul of thought.

BREVIESCA.   Well, take the soul, but we will keep **to**
sense.

          (FONSECA *nods at him approvingly.*)

DIEGO. There's many a joke had better not be
    cracked.
  The kernel's rot.
BREVIESCA.   You're free, sir, with your tongue.
FONSECA. Yes, too free for a stranger.
JAMES.   Come, come, come.
    Enthusiasm needs a margin.
FONSECA.   But
  We may not need enthusiasm.
JAMES.   What ?—
    And you say this ?—a priest ?
BREVIESCA.   And, pray, why not ?
JAMES. Why not ?—Why, friend, enthusiasm is
    The essence of religion——
DIEGO.   Nothing worth
  With the uplift and the oversight.
  That wanting, 'tis a minor quantity
  Whose measure's not in worth but lack of it.
                (*to* JAMES.)
    Not true ?
JAMES.   I think your training has been good.
DIEGO. Yes, I have known Columbus.
FELIPA (*to* CORREO).   How I wish
  That I had known him !
CORREO.   You ?
FELIPA.   Why, any man (*pointing to* DIEGO)
  To kindle fire like that——
CORREO.   Must have enough
  To keep a maiden warm and cosy, eh ?—

Think you that follows always? I've known men
Whose thought would flash like lightning, lighting
   up
Half heaven besides the whole of earth ; and yet
A whirlwind, did you trust to its caress,
Would never lead you in a madder dance.

DIEGO. I said I knew Columbus. One less mad
Does not exist.

FONSECA.   Oh, you've been bit by him !

JAMES. Come, come, the church is wise, perhaps, to
   put
Her break on wheels that else would whirl us
   down,
But how about those wheels when mounting up ?

*Enter—Left Center—*COLUMBUS.

DIEGO. He's coming now. He'll speak too for
   himself.
   (*Rising and extending hand to* COLUMBUS.)
Good-day.

COLUMBUS (*aside*). You here, Diego ?

DIEGO (*aside to* COLUMBUS). Yes, but no one knows
That I'm your brother. Better so, perhaps.

COLUMBUS. I see—can help me more.

JAMES (*rising with the rest at the tables and moving toward* COLUMBUS). Good-day.
      (*Introducing* COLUMBUS.)
                  Our friends,
The Dona Correo,—Felipa, Don

Fonseca, Breviesca, Correo—
Like you a sailor of experience.
       (*All bow, as do also* FONSECA *and* BREVIESCA.)
COLUMBUS (*to ladies and* CORREO).   It gives me joy
       to meet you.
CORREO.   We'll sit down?
   (*All sit from left to right in this order :* COLUMBUS,
          DIEGO, DOÑA CORREO, CORREO. FELIPA,
          JAMES, BREVIESCA *and* FONSECA.)
JAMES. You come here every day. I hear?
COLUMBUS.   Almost.
JAMES. You're making up for time you lost at sea?
COLUMBUS. Yes, making up and mounting up. I like
       The uplift of the services.
JAMES (*to* FONSECA). There, there,
       Fonseca, one point scored against yourself!
       Don't dull the blade that carves at your own feast.
                 (*to* COLUMBUS *in explanation.*)
       Oh, nothing serious !—an argument
       About good churchmen, and enthusiasts.
COLUMBUS. I see—and me. Yet we've been told
          to preach
       The truth to all the world.
                     (*to* FONSECA.)
                          You think 'tis done?
       Besides, I'm not a mere enthusiast.
BREVIESCA. And yet would sail across the unknown
       sea.
COLUMBUS. I would.

BREVIESCA. But that ——

COLUMBUS. I have good reasons for.

FONSECA. And where, pray, do you find them?

COLUMBUS. Everywhere —
Without a single fact against them.

BREVIESCA. Ha,
Without a single fact!

COLUMBUS. Well, name one, then.

BREVIESCA. Enough for me, if one could cross the
sea.
We should have found it out.

COLUMBUS. So?—How?

DIEGO (*to* BREVIESCA). No, no:
The world has had too many men like you.

FONSECA. And well for its own good! If lands
were there,
The Lord would let us know it.

COLUMBUS. There are lands
Men have not known.

FONSECA. And that would make you brave
The blazing waves, and have your ship burned up?

COLUMBUS. Ten years ago, the waters just beyond
Cape Bojador were said to burn thus: now
Men sail them, far as Cape de Vere.

FELIPA. That's true.

COLUMBUS. And they return with branches, leaves
and flowers
That float from further west: and you have read
The ancients?

BREVIESCA.   Yes, about Atlantis, yes;
  But that was lost.—You'll find it easy enough.
  'Tis done by sinking.

FONSECA.   Ha, ha, ha, well said!

COLUMBUS.   Oh, there are other tales! Late travelers
        too,
  Like Marco Polo and John Mandeville——

FONSECA.   Now, pardon me; but stick, man, to
        your text.
  It was of facts that you began to speak——

COLUMBUS.   And that which gives them value.

BREVIESCA.   Fancies, eh?

COLUMBUS.   Not fact-full only, but a mind that you
  Deem fanciful, is needed, would a man
  Put this and that together, and build up
  The only structure that can make his facts
  Worth knowing.

JAMES (rising). True as gospel that!   But now
  I must be going.   (to COLUMBUS.)
                    You will come with me?—
  Another map—we'll talk of it.   Besides,
  Prince Henry will be there to-day.

BREVIESCA (rising, to COLUMBUS).   Ay, ay;
  He'll let you sail your ship up to the moon,
  As mad as you are!

FONSECA (rising, to BREVIESCA).   Good! I like you,
        man,
  You have some sense.

CORREO (aside, to JAMES).   The Prince believes in
  him?

JAMES. If not in him, at least in enterprise.

COLUMBUS (*to* JAMES). 'Tis just the meeting I had
    prayed to have.
 Too good in you to further it! I'll come.

CORREO (*to* COLUMBUS). We'll see you soon at our
    home too, I hope?

BREVIESCA (*aside*). At their home—what? Columbus
    and not me?

COLUMBUS (*to* CORREO). I'm very busy and have
    little time——

FELIPA (*to* COLUMBUS). But we have maps my
    father made ; and these
 You might find helpful.

COLUMBUS (*to* FELIPA). Thank you. I will come.
    Good-day.

FELIPA *and* DONA CORREO. Good-day.

  (COLUMBUS *and* JAMES *exchange bows with all.*)

       *Exeunt—Left—*COLUMBUS *and* JAMES.

CORREO (*to* FELIPA *and* DONA CORREO). But we
    too must be going.

    They bow to those that are left on stage. Ex-
    *eunt—Right—*CORREO, FELIPA *and* DONA
    CORREO, *followed by* FONSECA.

DIEGO (*to* BREVIESCA). Ah, Breviesca, even you'll
    admit
 Enthusiasm has been king to-day ;—
 Within a single hour thrown wide apart
  2

The palace bars, and parlor doors that guard
The prettiest girl in Portugal.

BREVIESCA.   Oh, yes!
But wait you till the end comes.

DIEGO.   In the end,
As the beginning, nothing thrives but spirit.
I'll trust to its survival every time.
A prince——

BREVIESCA.   Is mortal.

DIEGO.   He's a lord of earth;
And on the earth he sometimes has the power
To make a man immortal.

BREVIESCA.   Humph! 'Tis strange
You like that egotist—insufferable!

DIEGO. Why, no. 'Tis you that are insufferable
I mean to him.   He dreams of destiny.
His soul is in his work.   'Tis that that speaks,
And like a sovereign.   Soul is always sovereign.

BREVIESCA. One's destiny, you think, is made by
talk?

DIEGO.   One's destiny was never yet fulfilled
By one whose coward conscience dared not give
Expression to the spirit that inspired it.

   *Exeunt—Right—*BREVIESCA *and* DIEGO.

SCENE SECOND. —*Parlor in the house of* DONA CORREO *and* FELIPA *at Lisbon. Entrances at Right Side and Left Side.*

*Enter—Right—*DONA CORREO *and* FELIPA *in out-door dresses, as in last Act.*

FELIPA.   I feared that we should not be back.
    You know
  Columbus will be here to day.   They say
  He's sure now to succeed.

D. CORREO.   I have my doubts.

FELIPA.   Prince Henry's promised him ——

D. CORREO.   Prince Henry's ill.
  I'm sorry, though, that I can't stay with you.
  Give my excuses, please—ay, ay, and yours.—
  Breviesca's coming too.

FELIPA.   Oh, that man, humph!

D. CORREO.   We all accept his suit.

FELIPA.   Except the one
  That should be suited

D. CORREO.   Whom we all so trust,
  We trust, too, in her wisdom.
               (Kissing FELIPA.)
                    With Columbus
  Be not too cordial.

FELIPA.   Not too cordial?

D. CORREO.   No.
  Cordialities that make the backward friends

But tempt the forward to presumption.   Force,
Prepared to clear its own approaches, flouts
A welcome meant for weakness.

FELIPA.   He's not forward.

D. CORREO.   A civil man enough !   But then they
   say——

FELIPA.   The one that everybody's bid can bind
Is everybody's bondsman.

D. CORREO.   But I know
The neighbors——

FELIPA.   And I know myself.   'Tis wise
To make it mistress of my choice, I think.

D. CORREO.   Now, now, fair play !   Fair play in
   argument,
Will catch our thoughts before it throws them
  back.
They say he's flighty.

FELIPA.   So are birds—and so
Are—angels——

D. CORREO.   What ?

FELIPA.   And every kind of life
Above the common.

D. CORREO.   Why, my girl !
One might suppose——
    (*Looking toward window at right.*)
     But see !   He comes.   I'll go.
Be on your guard—and think.   Good-bye.
    (*Kissing her.*)
   *Exit—Left—*DONA CORREO.

FELIPA (*to herself*).   And think?—
  I need that caution?—when this beaker all
        (*Placing her hand on her heart.*)
  Is brimming to its overflow?—And think?—
  When every thought is radiant with his form
  Like surging sea-waves glancing back the sun?—
  Enter—Right - COLUMBUS *carrying a roll of maps.*
  Good-day, Columbus.
COLUMBUS.   It was good enough
  For me before you called it so.
FELIPA.   With all
  Your disappointments? Then 'tis true. Prince
        Henry——
COLUMBUS. Has promised all I wish. I shall
        succeed.
(*They sit together on sofa, while* COLUMBUS *hands her
        the maps.*)
FELIPA. Thank God !
COLUMBUS.   Ay, ay ! Oh, I have sailed in nights,
  Dark nights, and thanked Him for a single star
  To guide me. Now I've two—the Prince and
        you.
FELIPA (*unrolling the maps and looking at one*).
  You do me too much honor.
COLUMBUS.   Could I ? Nay.
  A soul that summons all that does one's best
  To do still better, sits upon a throne
  Than which none higher is conceivable.
FELIPA. I was not conscious——

COLUMBUS.   Nay, nor is a child
   Of aught in her of movement or of form,
   That, fitting sweet ideals of loveliness,
   Makes fancied grace and beauty visible.
FELIPA (*looking down at the map*). And yet, I had
       not thought my father's maps——
COLUMBUS. Ay, they confirm twice over all my
       plan—
   Not they alone, but your directions with them.
FELIPA. Mine? (*Sitting with one hand resting on
       the map.*)
COLUMBUS. Yes, your fingers pointing out the course.
   It's all of it just there, beneath your hand.
   A sailor steers the way his compass points.
FELIPA. (*Looking down at her hand on the map*).
   Is that your compass?
COLUMBUS.   It might compass me—
   I mean my soul.
FELIPA.   That little hand? Oh, what
   A little soul!
COLUMBUS.   Do souls have size? One might
   Be universed in this; yet not contained
                (*Pointing to her hand.*)
   In all the universe outside of it.
FELIPA. To put your soul thus in another's hand,—
   Would that be wise?
COLUMBUS.   Why not?—the hand that serves
   The soul one loves may serve but selfishly,
   And yet serve best the one that trusts to it.
FELIPA. But should it fetter him?

COLUMBUS.   'Twould give him joy
  In every atom of his frame to feel
  Its fingers' throb and pressure.
FELIPA.   Would not bound
  Away?
COLUMBUS.   Away and up, but always back again,
  Like grains of sand in earthquakes.
FELIPA.   Foolish man!
COLUMBUS.   Why, only God is wholly wise; and I,
  I'm but a man—so never quite so manly
  As when—why, say—made foolish.
FELIPA (*rising, as does also* COLUMBUS).
                         Some one comes.

  Enter—Right a SERVANT, *bringing a note.*

FELIPA.   A note for me—from whom?—
          (*Opening and reading the note.*)

          *Exit—Right—*SERVANT.
                         Can this be true?
  Bad news for us, Columbus, very bad!—
  Prince Henry's dead.
COLUMBUS.   Prince Henry? What?—No, no!
FELIPA.   It must be so. You see who sent it look.
  (*Handing the note to* COLUMBUS, *who reads it.*)
COLUMBUS.   Impossible! Heaven cannot be mali-
    cious.
  What? build so high a structure for my hope,
  Then knock the prop from under? All, all gone?
FELIPA.   There may be others.
COLUMBUS.   May be?—There are none,

FELIPA.   But you have me still.

COLUMBUS.   Ah, that's it.   We must
   Forget all this—at least for years and years.—
   Oh, I know what it means !   I've seen years like
      them.

FELIPA.   Forget all this ?

COLUMBUS.   You do not understand.
   Prince Henry was my patron.   Backed by him,
   Success was possible.   I felt I trod
   An equal plane with other of your suitors :
   But now I'm worse off than a beggar.

FELIPA.   No !
   You have your pencil—still can draw——

COLUMBUS.   Yet not
   The outlines I had hoped—of that new land,
   And you, its princess.   No : there looms a face
   With more care-lines upon its wrinkled brow
   Than e'er I blacked a map with.

FELIPA.   There are ships
   That still need captains.

COLUMBUS.   Could one see their sails
   Like arms, white-surpliced, praying heaven for
      wind,
   Yet ever turn his prow away from that
   Which he had vowed to heaven that he would seek ?

FELIPA.   But you can wait—you're so strong !—
      you can wait——

COLUMBUS.   I can—but you—no, no : where hope
   still shines

There's joy in pain and death is glorious;
But where no ray of hope is visible,
To wait is full damnation.

FELIPA.   You say this?—
  I thought——-

COLUMBUS.   Oh, I !—yes, I can wait forever.
  The light's within me.   But can you see through
  These forms that cloak it, worse than worst of rags,
  Discourtesy, suspicion and contempt
  Of those who know Columbus as the fool?

FELIPA.   But——

COLUMBUS.   No, deny it not.   I know it, feel it.
  Your mother, sister, brother—yes, I grant
  They tolerate me; but when patronless
  And penniless, 'twill be a different tale.

FELIPA.   Nay, nay; that cannot be!   They'll feel
    with me
  How noble 'tis to be a man like you——

COLUMBUS.   A pauper and fanatic——

FELIPA.   No, a man
  Who, all alone, can stand with but one friend,
  His own brave soul, and trample underfoot
  A hissing world that, coiling like a snake,
  Would clutch him to its clod and hold him there.

COLUMBUS.   Too much!   To-day you think it, but
    to-morrow--
  Next year—in ten years——No, I have no right
  To put you to the test.   No, let me go—
  Farewell.

FELIPA. Will you fare quite as well without me?

COLUMBUS. Felipa, nay, it cannot be.

FELIPA. You think
A woman's heart, if tested through long years,
With burdening love would break?—'tis kindlier
To break it at the start?

*Enter—Right—*BREVIESCA.

COLUMBUS (*not observing* BREVIESCA). Felipa, no—
A faith like yours—my God, what shall I do?
I would not harm you, yet have done the harm.

BREVIESCA (*sarcastically to the two*). Ah, so!—I see
that I'm too late—

FELIPA (*aside, anxiously, to* COLUMBUS). Except
For one thing.—Save me.

COLUMBUS (*to* BREVIESCA). We're betrothed.

*Exit, with sarcastic bow—Right—*BREVIESCA.
*Exeunt—Left—*FELIPA *and* COLUMBUS.

SCENE THIRD.— *Working room in the house of* COLUM-
BUS. *Maps and charts, hanging on the walls, and
lying on a large table at Back Center : also books,
instruments for navigation, and implements for meas-
uring and drawing. Window at Right. Entrances at Right Side Rear and Left Side.*

Enter—Right—a MAID *and a* WOMAN, *followed by
other Women.*

WOMAN. Columbus home?

MAID.   No.

WOMAN.   What's he doing now ?

MAID.   Oh, just the same as ever !

WOMAN.   Nothing, eh ?

(*To the other Women, who have remained near the door.*)
    Come in.   (*to* MAID.)

                        We thought that we should like to
                        see——

(*Handling charts and implements on the table.*)

MAID.   You really shouldn't touch them.

WOMAN.   No ?   Why not ?

MAID.   He wouldn't like it.

WOMAN.   Oh, of course not ! but
    He's never violent, is he ?—

                        (*Pointing to a chart.*)

                        What a blotch !

MAID.   A chart, you know.

WOMAN.   A chart ?—A chart of what ?
    I never saw a chart like that—looks like
    A crazy quilt.   And so he wastes his time
    On things like these ?—Felipa dying too !
    No wonder !—Think of it !—Ten mortal years
    Of this, and no one knows what more.   At night,
    I wouldn't dare to stay alone with him,
    Would you ?—say, would you ?

MAID.   Why !   I—no—he never——

WOMAN.   Of course not.   You would be afraid, of
        course.
    I had a cousin once who went insane.

And all his family had to play insane
To keep him company. 'Twas royal sport
Till, sure that he was royal and they slaves,
He ordered off their heads.

MAID.   And then?

WOMAN.   And then
They left off playing, and made war in earnest;
And so dethroned him. They should do so here;
The sooner, too, the better! Look at this:
           (*Taking up a sharp instrument.*)
Not safe in hands like his!
           (*Knocking at the door at the Right.*)
                         Hark, hark! What's that?
It can't be he? Say, you can let us out
                (*Starting for Left.*)
The other door, not so?

MAID.   No need of that!
'Tis no one but the tailor.

WOMAN.   Sure of it?
  (*Crossing room and looking out window at Right.*)

MAID. Comes every day.

WOMAN.   What for?

MAID.   To bid us think
Of Adam's fall that made us civilized,
Wear clothes, and bear the curse of paying for
    them.
           (*Opening door at Right.*)
    *Enter—Right—*TAILOR, *to whom she speaks.*
   He's out.

TAILOR.   Oh, yes, I know.   He's always out—
      Out of his head at least.   Were he but out
      My breeches, 'twould be better.   Left no word?
MAID.   He bade me say that he expects the king ——
TAILOR.   If all the kings that are expected came,
      There's none would have a kingdom.   Ugh !   I'll
          strip
      And cage his bareness for a jail-show.   Ugh !
MAID.   But, really, he is honest.   He expects——

          Enter—Right Side—suddenly, the GROCER.

GROCER.   Tell him his expectations are too old.
      Fresh expectations, like fresh eggs, may hatch.
      Not so with stale ones, though, however white.
WOMAN (*turning from window at Right, where she has
          been looking out, and gazing at the* GROCER).
      The grocer, eh ?
                    (*Speaking to the other women.*)
                                        And all the family
      Are coming now—Columbus too.   I saw them.
      There'll be a scene here.   I prefer the back-
          ground.

          *Exit—Left—*WOMAN, *followed by the other Women.*

TAILOR (*to* GROCER).
      Let's club together, friend—I mean let fly
      Our blows at him together—down him sooner !
GROCER (*to* MAID, *and holding a paper toward her*).
      I can't fulfill this order.

MAID.   But you must.
  It's for his wife.
GROCER.   I can't afford, myself,
  To keep a wife.
TAILOR.   Still less when keeping his.

*Enter—Right—*DONA CORREO *and* CORREO *pushing*
    FELIPA *in a chair upon wheels.*

MAID (*to* GROCER).
  His wife is ill. You would not let her die?
GROCER.   Not I, but he; and there are other
          shops——
MAID.   He's tried them all.
GROCER.   Then let him try the jail.
  They'll feed him there, or sell him out.
DONA CORREO.   What's that?
GROCER (*pointing toward charts and implements on
          table*).   He ought to sell these things and pay
  us off.
DONA CORREO.   Not paid you yet? Oh, well, you
  may be right!
FELIPA (*to* D. CORREO).   They may be right?
  Why, this would ruin him.
DONA CORREO (*to* FELIPA).   Not outside things that
  men can take away
  Bring ruin, but the things that stay within,
  Which would they could take!
            (*To* GROCER *and* TAILOR.)
                  Look you —there he comes.

*Enter—Right—*COLUMBUS.

COLUMBUS (*to* GROCER *and* TAILOR). Well, gentlemen?

TAILOR (*holding his bill toward* COLUMBUS). I've
brought your bill.

GROCER. And I.

TAILOR. We say an honest man———

COLUMBUS (*motioning toward* FELIPA). But not,
please, now.
My wife is ill.

TAILOR (*pointing toward the table*). We say—your
sister too—
An honest man would sell these traps: not let
His creditors go begging.

GROCER. Ay, or come so.

(*appealing to* FELIPA.)
You think it too.

(*to* COLUMBUS.)
You see it in her face.

TAILOR (*half aside*). Oh, he sees nothing! Give
one's brain a whack.
It flies from earth to stars. They're all in here.
(*pointing to his head.*)

COLUMBUS (*referring to implements on table*). These
are the tools I work with, gentlemen.

GROCER. Humph, they work poorly, better give
them up!

COLUMBUS. The king——

TAILOR.   'Tis ten years since we heard of him.

COLUMBUS.   Your bill's but three months old.

TAILOR.   I spoke of hearing.

COLUMBUS.   The present king has not been on the
        throne
    But——

GROCER.   Every king's the same to us —and you,
    You'll find.

COLUMBUS.   Wait, gentlemen ——

TAILOR.   We've learned that lesson.

COLUMBUS.   My brothers will be here to-day.

TAILOR.   And then?

COLUMBUS.   You'll find that I'm in favor at the
        court.

TAILOR.   If so?

COLUMBUS.   'Twill send me what will outpay more
    Than twenty score of times your paltry bills.
    What say you?

GROCER.   Well, we'll wait, perhaps.   Fact is,
    'Tis hard to break old habits.
                    (*to* TAILOR.)
                        Shall we, eh?

(TAILOR *bows in acquiescence.* GROCER *continues to*
                COLUMBUS.)

    But see we get what balances our claim,
    Or else we'll weigh these things against them yet,
                (*Pointing to the table.*)
    And sell them too by weight.

        *Exeunt—Right Side—*GROCER *and* TAILOR.

COLUMBUS.   No doubt they will.
'Tis common in the judgments of this world
For worth to yield to weight.
DONA CORREO.   'Tis a disgrace—
A scene like this in my own sister's house!
FELIPA.   Why, sister, when the king——
DONA CORREO.   Oh, dear, you know
The king's a fiction, like all else that's here.
FELIPA.   But yet the king took interest in his charts,
And sent for them.
DONA CORREO.   Ay, ay, and found out so—
'Tis likely now—that he can't draw at all—
Except from his own fancy.   Who wants that?
A visionary man produces visions;
And in the world that is, men want what is.
COLUMBUS.   Why, madam, I am accurate.
DONA CORREO.   Perhaps.
Who knows it though?   Yourself?   If one besides,
You're not the great discoverer that you deem.
And if there's no one knows it, all must judge
By what they hear.   What do they hear of you?
CORREO.   Humph. I can tell.
                    (*to* COLUMBUS.)
                    Forgive me: but 'tis time
You knew the truth.   I thought, perhaps, to lease
A ship that you could sail,--make money by,
But——
DONA CORREO.   Been too long from practice?
CORREO.   No, no; worse!

3

Dona Correo.   Is such an idler, as they think ?
Correo.   Worse yet—
  A man who can't be trusted, sure to do
  The wrong thing for the right.
Columbus.   And you say that ?
Correo.   Not I, but those that give you reputation.
Columbus.   Am I to blame ?
Correo.   Who else is, pray ? They say
  That you would sail but heaven alone knows
        where.
  And I confess, I half believe you would.
Felipa   Oh brother !
Columbus (*aside to* Correo).   Cruel, talking thus to
        her !
                    (*to* Felipa.)
  The other room will be far better, dear,
  Than this.   'Tis nothing !—They exaggerate.
  They hurt my feelings ? Oh, why, why, why, why,
  You never saw a fisher catch a fish
  Whose bait would not get tangled in the line.
  Just wait.   I'll get the better of them yet.
  You trust to me.   There, dear.
        (*Gesturing to* Maid *to wheel* Felipa.)
                        I'm coming soon.

*Exeunt—Left—*Maid *wheeling* Felipa *in her chair.*

Dona Correo (*to* Correo).   You're right.   The
        time has come to tell him truth.
        (*To* Columbus *and gesturing toward* Correo.)

You think him cruel. What are you, yourself?
(*Pointing toward the Left.*)
See what ten years of this have made of her?
I come, and find her wanting everything—
Food, physic, nearly dying at your hands.
COLUMBUS. No, no: do not say that.
DONA CORREO.   I will. 'Tis time.
COLUMBUS. She still believes in me.
DONA CORREO.   As infidels
In their Mohammed, and are cursed for it.
COLUMBUS. I think that you forget. How many
    men
Of humble, foreign birth demand and get
A summons to an audience with the king?
Say that of such importance that the king,
To weigh it, calls his wisest counselors?
Who argue it for days, with some, at least,
Upon his side whom you think stands alone?
DONA CORREO. How many on his side?
COLUMBUS.   Enough to make
The king request his charts—the work of years
That you think wasted.
DONA CORREO.   'Twas five months ago;
And nothing's come of them.
COLUMBUS.   There's too much life
In truth of any sort, to let me doubt
That where 'tis sown 'twill grow. 'Tis a begin-
    ning.
DONA CORREO. A very small one.

COLUMBUS.   And a seed is so,
  Whose growth's enormous. When one waits the
    dawn,
  A flush is better than a flash, which oft
  But bodes a rush-light.

*Enter—Right—*DIEGO *and* BARTHOLOMEW, *to whom*
    COLUMBUS *now turns.*

                 Ah, they come at last !—
My brothers, welcome !
DIEGO (*to* COLUMBUS).
               So to you.
      (*to* DONA CORREO *and* CORREO.)
                     And you.

BARTHOLOMEW.   And all.
        (*All greet each other.*)
COLUMBUS (*to* DIEGO).   You bring me news?
DIEGO.   Ay, by and by.
     (*Glancing at* DONA C. *and* CORREO.)
COLUMBUS (*to* DONA C. *and* CORREO).   You will ex-
   cuse us?
D. CORREO.   Certainly.
     *Exeunt—Left—*DONA C. *and* CORREO.
COLUMBUS (*to* DIEGO).   This news?
DIEGO (*sadly*). My brother, can you bear it?
COLUMBUS.   I have borne
  With many things.
DIEGO.   You've been misunderstood,
  Misjudged, maligned ; but all were less than this.

COLUMBUS.   How so ?

BARTHOLOMEW.   The king——

COLUMBUS.   He has not sent the money ?

BARTHOLOMEW.   The money ?

COLUMBUS.   Yes, his agent promised it.

BARTHOLOMEW.   We had not thought you cared so
    much for that.

COLUMBUS.   Not I, but these—my wife, my family.
  The king sent here requesting all details.
  It took me weeks to draft them, had to turn
  My methods upside down and inside out,
  And mass and microscope and magnify,
  Till truth was large enough for all to see it.
  Meantime, what gaze had I to fix upon
  My earnings ?   So they fled, and now——

DIEGO.   I see.
  No watch-dog keeps a creditor at bay
  Like well-housed earnings.—But we've heard no
    talk
  Of pay.

COLUMBUS.   When it was clearly promised ?—what ?
  Then I, who trusted in the royal word
  And gave it currency, am made for this
  A charlatan who trades upon a cheat ?

DIEGO.   And worse.   He's kept your charts.

COLUMBUS.   He's kept them ?—Why—
  With truth, the longer kept, the longer thought of ;
  And thinking feeds conviction.   On my soul,
  The king will let me sail yet.   You shall see.

BARTHOLOMEW.   Oh no, not you !

COLUMBUS.   Not me, not me ?—and why ?

DIEGO.   My brother, all your draughts, your work
       for years
   Rest like a charter in another's hands.
   His powers are piloting to-day a ship
   That's pointed toward the west ; his head's de-
       creed
   To wear the wreath for what your own conceived.

COLUMBUS.   Impossible !

DIEGO.   I'm sure of it.

BARTHOLOMEW.   And I,
   I know his pilot—not a firm man though !
   He'll never cross the sea.

COLUMBUS.   I could prefer
   He should, than by a failure earn my scheme
   Discredit.

DIEGO.   Which he surely will.

COLUMBUS.   Too true !

DIEGO.   Oh, curse the king !

COLUMBUS.   Could you have conceived
   Such baseness ?

DIEGO.   Don't ask me.   I'm not the devil.

COLUMBUS.   What reasons could he have ?

DIEGO.   Enough of them
   In such a world as this.   You've genius, brains ;
   And those without them must get even with you,
   If not by higher then by lower means.
   You are original and they derived ;

And thought that's centered in itself, owns not
A parentage that puts another first.
And you're a foreigner, they Portuguese.

COLUMBUS. But such dishonor in a king!

DIEGO. Why not?
A king is human ; place is relative ;
Dishonor's honor when true honor's down.
Make men in common kneel, and common men
Stand up like giants. Banish out of sight
The bright minds, and the dull ones beam like
beacons.

(*A knocking is heard at the Right Side Entrance.*)

Enter—Left—the MAID.

MAID. My master?

COLUMBUS (*to* MAID). Well?

MAID. Your wife desires to see you.

COLUMBUS. Yes, presently. There's some one at
the door.

*Exit—Right—*MAID.

(COLUMBUS *continues to the brothers.*)

If 'twere not for my wife here, I should leave
This Portugal forever.

BARTHOLOMEW. 'Twould be well.

COLUMBUS. There certainly is elsewhere enterprise
With honesty. I think that I should try
The court of England. There's a land with men
White skinned, the spirit just behind the face,
Their very faults the proof that they're not false ;
Too impudent for truthlessness, too bold

To stab behind one's back, too proud of push
To trip with little tricks, too fond of sport
To keep one down, when down.

BARTHOLOMEW.   I might try it.

COLUMBUS.   You might and would, Bartholomew?

BARTHOLOMEW.   I will.

*Enter—Right—*MAID.

COLUMBUS (*to* MAID).   A visitor?

MAID.   A message from the king,

DIEGO.   We knew 'twas coming.   Now you are
   prepared.

COLUMBUS.   My soul demands in one whom I obey.
   A moral equal, at the least.   It comes
   In vain.

(*To* MAID.)

   And messengers?

MAID.   Yes.

COLUMBUS.   Show them in.

*Exit—Right—*MAID.   *The eyes of* COLUMBUS
   *follow her, and look through the door, which
   she leaves ajar.*

Breviesca?   He alone makes both of them
Birds of most evil omen.

*Enter—Right—*BREVIESCA *and another man, attended by* MAID, *who exits at Left.   All bow.*
                          Gentlemen?—
And will you sit?
   (*He motions towards seats.   Their manner in-
   dicates refusal, and they remain standing.*)

BREVIESCA.   I thank you, no.   The king
  Has sent requesting you to visit him.
COLUMBUS.   Requesting me to visit him?   For what?
BREVIESCA.   Your charts.—He would examine them
    with you.
COLUMBUS.   With what intent?
BREVIESCA.   To satisfy you— —
COLUMBUS.   Me?
  Tell him I'm satisfied remaining here.
BREVIESCA.   But he demands your presence.
COLUMBUS.   Oh, demands!
  'Tis not for my sake, then—for his, you come.
  You've brought me then the means with which to
    go?
BREVIESCA.   How so?
COLUMBUS.   The money? or conveyance?
BREVIESCA.   What?
COLUMBUS.   I need the one or other.
DIEGO.   Certainly.
BREVIESCA.   But when the king demands——
COLUMBUS.   I have demands
  That antedate the king's.   He promised me
  A sum of money for my charts.   Where is it?
BREVIESCA.   You dare dispute the royal will?
COLUMBUS.   I dare
  Dispute what you impute to royal honor.

     *Enter—Left—*MAID, *evidently in distress.*

MAID.   My master?

COLUMBUS.   Why, what is it?

MAID.   She—seems—dying.

COLUMBUS.   What, what? my wife?

    (*Starts for the door—Left—*BREVIESCA *makes a gesture of disapproval.*)

BREVIESCA.   Give us your answer first.

COLUMBUS.   You press this now?

BREVIESCA.   We represent the king.
Do you forget that he must be supreme?

COLUMBUS.   I do in presence of a Higher King.
Oh God, had he but kept his word with me
This had not happened!

      *Exeunt—Left—*COLUMBUS *and the* MAID.

BREVIESCA (*bowing sarcastically to* DIEGO *and* BAR-
    THOLOMEW).   So we shall report.

    (*Exeunt—Right—*BREVIESCA *and other man.*

BARTHOLOMEW.   Diego, if the king excuse this
    yet——

DIEGO.   His creditors who hear of it will not.

    (*Pointing toward Left.*)

If she be flown, I fear we all must fly.

BARTHOLOMEW.   But why should he so suffer!—I
    half think
There's that in truth to spirit which makes all
The world its enemy.

DIEGO.   Yet conquers it.

      CURTAIN.   END OF ACT I.

ACT SECOND.

SCENE FIRST :—*A Spanish camp by night, illumed by distant red camp-fires. Backing at the Left a royal tent with curtains before its entrance. To the sides at right of stage, connecting with Right Side Second Entrance, the tent of* COLUMBUS, *its curtains drawn aside revealing a cot or lounge on which two or more can sit, also a chair or two. Just outside the same tent on the side toward the center of stage, a log on which two or more can sit. To the sides at Left of stage, trees. Entrances at the Left Center through the royal tent: at the Right Side Rear, behind the tent of* COLUMBUS*: at the Right Side through his tent: at the Right Side Front, between it and the audience: and at the Left Side, Rear and Front through trees.*

Enter—Left—a MOOR.

MOOR.   Darkness for deeds of darkness !   Thank
         the stars,
I've almost reached the queen's pavilion ; yet
In all this Christian camp, blood-red as life,
Not one suspects the Moor—this heathen worm
Who's wriggled to it's core.   Her tent !—steal in !
(*Addressing his steel dirk as he looks at it, then lifts it
                 upward.*)
Ay, that's my motto : Steel in, till you start

The spirit of the queen, steel it away.
Hark!—some one's coming.—I must hide.—Aha!
  (*Looks around, then apparently hides himself
    in the folds of the canvas at the Back Side
    of the tent of* COLUMBUS.)
Convenient folds these!—Thank you, Christian
  friends.

Exit the MOOR *—Right—behind the tent of*
  COLUMBUS.

Enter—Right—through this tent, DIEGO *and* COLUM-
  BUS, *dressed as a soldier.*

  (*The two are at first inside the tent: but, as
    they talk, they gradually come out onto the
    stage in front of it.*)
COLUMBUS. You've heard from England and Bar-
  tholomew?
DIEGO. I have.
COLUMBUS.   And his success?
DIEGO.   They thought us fools.
  And how fared you in Genoa and Venice?
COLUMBUS. They knew we were. I half believe
  that flight
Was all that saved me from a mad-house. Oh,
The world's a tyrant to the soul would serve it.
It treats him like a female relative
Whose drudgery is deemed supremely paid
By her own love. But when the wage one wants
Is not within one, love's not paid at all.

DIEGO.   Yes, yes ; I fear you'll have to give it up.

COLUMBUS.   My voyage ?

DIEGO.   Yes.

COLUMBUS.   Not till I die ; and that
   I'll do as soon as hope dies out of me.

DIEGO.   But you've enlisted here ?

COLUMBUS.   It helps me on.
   Men judge of us by standards in themselves :
   And so like us when they see us like them.
   Kings take to tales, too, writ with points like
        this—
        (*Pointing, with a gesture, to his sword.*)
   "Twill underscore " your humble servant " when
   He signs his next request.

        Enter—Left Side—at the Rear two young
        OFFICERS. *They stand looking at* COLUM-
        BUS *and* DIEGO, *making signs to indicate
        that they consider* COLUMBUS *out of his
        mind.* COLUMBUS *notices them.*

DIEGO.   You've met the king ?

COLUMBUS.   I'm waiting for a chance——

DIEGO.   It promises ?
   What seem your prospects ?

COLUMBUS (*pointing to the officers*).
                     Watch those men and see.
   We use sign-language here.   Theirs means " Co-
        lumbus."
   The women, children, all have learned it, too,
   And point it now and then with exclamations.

DIEGO (*glancing angrily at the men*).   Outrageous ! I
  will stop them.
COLUMBUS (*staying him with his hand*).   Why, what
  use ?
  "Tis better to be made a laughing stock,
  Than have men take in us no stock at all.
DIEGO.   Do you say this, who were so sensitive,
  High-spirited ?

  (*The Officers cross the stage and Exeunt at the
  Right Rear.*)

COLUMBUS.   One may have so much sense
  It holds the spirit down.   Besides, our spheres
  Are stagnant and need movement.   Make men
    take
  You gravely if you can : if not, what though
  They laugh ?   They're moved in that way.   There
    are times
  The tiniest tinkles that can shake the air
  Ring up life's curtain for its grandest act.
DIEGO.   You talk like one that's lost all friends.
COLUMBUS.   Why so ?
  "Tis light that trails a shade.   "Tis those with
    friends
  Are sure of foes ; and only those with neither
  Are sure of neither.
DIEGO.   Then you have them ?
COLUMBUS.   Yes.
DIEGO.   What class of people ?

COLUMBUS.   Oh, both Dukes and Dons;
  And, to make life complete, at least one woman.
DIEGO. Aha!
COLUMBUS. The image of my lost Felipa.
DIEGO. You're then to marry?
COLUMBUS.   If I had the wish
  I could not have the will. Her family
  Are not agreeable——
DIEGO.   To you?
COLUMBUS.   To her,
  When seen with me; and—well!—enough
  For one man to have sacrificed one woman
  To appease what he esteems as God.
DIEGO.   How so?
COLUMBUS. A woman craves attention and a home.
  Her lover's mission, let it oft withdraw
  His ear or sphere from her, seems then her rival.
DIEGO. It would not, did she love the man's true
        self.
COLUMBUS. Mayhap, and yet the kinds of love men
        feel
  For mistress and for mission are so like!——
  What, if behind the mission's love should be
  Some sentient spirit too in realms unseen?
  These women may be right. They may have
        rivals.
  But what Felipa felt I could not help.
  Yet may avoid its repetition.
DIEGO (*doubtfully*).   Humph!

COLUMBUS. This one is but a sister, name more
    sacred
Than wife, I think, as wives go now.
DIEGO.   She thinks
    This too ?
COLUMBUS.   She should, and you?
DIEGO.   I think, perhaps,
    You ought to marry.
COLUMBUS.   Oh no! I have vowed
    Religiously—
DIEGO.   And might not be the first
    Religion led astray.
COLUMBUS.   Astray! how so?
DIEGO.   A brotherly or sisterly regard
    Grows up from family relationship.
    Train boys and girls together, side by side,
    As in one loyal household, holding all
    Humanity, and then perchance, may love's dis-
        honor
    Seem foul as incest, and imperilers of it,
    No longer vehicles of life humane,
    Unsouled of self-control, all flag themselves
    The death-trucks that they are, and make health
        scud
    From their contagion as from carrion.
COLUMBUS.   You mean——
DIEGO.   The young are not so trained in Spain—
    Not schooled to know each other, soul by soul;
    And nothing but the soul can outweigh sense.

COLUMBUS. In general, true !—but she——

DIEGO. Our lives reflect
The light of our surroundings. What are here ?—
Accursed customs that distrust the soul,
Ay, robe its every feature in their rags,
Each draped to hint deformity beneath.
Away with earthly habits that can hide
God's image framed within !

> *Enter—Left Side Front — the* MONK, JUAN
> PEREZ, *another* MONK, *the officer* SANCHEZ,
> *and several* SOLDIERS.

COLUMBUS (*looking toward the* MONK). Why, who
are these ?

PEREZ (*to* COLUMBUS).
God greet you friends.

COLUMBUS. His messengers are welcome.

PEREZ. And doubly so if from Jerusalem ?

COLUMBUS. The holy city ?

PEREZ. Yes. The grand Soldan
Of Egypt sent us.

COLUMBUS. With a message ?

PEREZ. Yes.
He vows that if the Spaniard will not stay
This war against the Moor, he'll rouse the East,
Pull down all Christian churches, and beneath
Entomb their worshipers.

COLUMBUS. He thinks this threat
Will influence Ferdinand ?

4

SANCHEZ.   It should not.
SOLDIER.   No.
COLUMBUS.   But must the faithful suffer?
PEREZ.   They do now.
    At each pretext oppressed, reviled, deprived
    Of property and freedom, flayed and hung,
    And heaven knows what : for it gets most of
        them.
SANCHEZ.   This should not be.
PEREZ.   Ah, when what should be is,
    What is will be beyond this earth.
SANCHEZ.   As soon
    As Spain's white line of ships have tailed for
      good,
    This flying kite of Africa, and cleared
    The blue about us, there should rest no ship
    Unarmed to right our brethren there.
SOLDIER.   Not one.
PEREZ (*to* SANCHEZ).   Would you go ?
SANCHEZ.   Ay, I would.
PEREZ.   The time may come   —
SANCHEZ (*to* SOLDIERS).
    Meanwhile, the Moor !   Now, to your stations —
    march.

*Exeunt—Right Side Rear—*SANCHEZ *and* SOLDIERS.

DIEGO (*glancing at the* MONKS, *and speaking aside to*
      COLUMBUS).
    They'll see the king—might speak for you, not so ?

COLUMBUS (*to* DIEGO). They might.

  (*To the* MONKS.) Perhaps you'll rest with us to-night?

PEREZ. We thank you—and your name?

  (*The* MONKS *and* DIEGO, *as* COLUMBUS *gestures to them, enter tent of* COLUMBUS *and sit.* COLUMBUS *sits on the log to the left of his tent with his back to center.*)

COLUMBUS.   Columbus.

PEREZ.   Oh!

  I've heard of you.

COLUMBUS.   Heard good?

PEREZ.   Why

COLUMBUS.   Ah, have not.

  I understand. The silence of the good

  Damns more than bad men's curses. Yet my aims

  Are one with yours—to speed the truth to all.

  But "all" means more than most men deem.

PEREZ.   The wise

  Aim not beyond their reach.

COLUMBUS.   The faithful aim

  Wherever they are called.

PEREZ.   You heard the call

  Just made?

COLUMBUS. And not a breast could out-thrill mine

  With indignation at the tale.

PEREZ.   It failed

  To stir your lip to pledges.

COLUMBUS.   When heaven crowns
  My present purpose——
PEREZ.   You'll be like your mates,
  Ennobled, rich, and found a family.
COLUMBUS. My western mission is for Christ
    alone.
  Pray heaven with me that I fulfill it; then
  I vow to live a life like yours, and more—·
  To give it to this eastern mission.   See—
(*Drawing his sword and showing the cross forming
          its hilt.*)
  This cross that aims the sword I wield. 'Twill
    find
  No final rest, till waved above the crescent.
PEREZ. You seem a holy man.

> *Enter —Left Center, from the royal tent,—
> BEATRIX, advances across the stage,
> touches COLUMBUS on his back, then with-
> draws toward Right Side Rear, behind his
> tent.*

COLUMBUS.   Nay, none is that.
  When men seem holy do not think of them,
  But of the cause that has affected them.
    (COLUMBUS *rises, as if looking for* BEATRIX.)
PEREZ (*to the other* MONK). He seems inspired to
    purposes well worth
  The world's regard.
OTHER MONK.   He does.

COLUMBUS (*aside as he looks behind him*).

                      What's this?—I think
I know. (*To* DIEGO) Diego, will you guide our
    friends
Across the pathway to the vacant tent?
There's one here who has business with me.

        Exeunt—Right—through the tent of COLUM-
       BUS, DIEGO *and the two* MONKS.

Enter—Right—from behind the same tent, BEATRIX.

COLUMBUS. You, Beatrix? and here?—this time of
    night?
Have you forgot? Your father——
BEATRIX.   Is a bird,
    Flown southward, wrong, forgetting for a time
    The winter whence it fled?
COLUMBUS.   But there are ways——
BEATRIX. I am not welcome then?
COLUMBUS.   Oh no— not that—
    But unexpected.
BEATRIX.   I have heard you say
    Good fortune would be so.
COLUMBUS.   You bring it, eh?
BEATRIX. One door ajar to it. These worthy
    friars,
    Just in your tent, I hear, will see the king.
    They might commend you.
COLUMBUS.   Yes, I thank you.
BEATRIX.   Well?

COLUMBUS.   How so?
BEATRIX.   You're cold.
COLUMBUS.   The night is.
BEATRIX.   I am not.
COLUMBUS.   No, no, forgive me.
BEATRIX.   I have more to say.
   The Dona Bobadilla— -
COLUMBUS.   Your old foe?
BEATRIX.   New friend: for your sake made and
    kept a friend
  By courtesies limbering my stiff limbs of pride
  Till limp and limping as humility.
COLUMBUS.   But really ——
BEATRIX.   Really, when one's inward sense
  Of mastership outweighs an outward show
  Of servitude, why, one but serves herself.
  This Dona Bobadilla has in mind
  To urge your claims upon the queen.
COLUMBUS.   She has?—
  What is it makes a woman serve like you
  A mere enthusiast without success?
BEATRIX.   That's better than to serve one with
    success.
COLUMBUS.   Why so?
BEATRIX.   It shows a spirit as it is.
  It throw's one's manhood into full relief,
  Stript of all circumstance and accident.
COLUMBUS.   This heart of mine were heavy were it
    not

Made light by eyes so bright as to detect
Beneath all veils disguising what it is,
Its one sole virtue.—You forget that all
The world is full of brains, and all the brains
Of whims, and all that gives the whims more worth
Than blood that churns them up to consciousness,
Is that they leave the brain and live in deeds.
Mine have not done this yet.

BEATRIX (*sitting on log to left of tent of Columbus, and
in doing so, letting the shawl that she has worn
fall from her on to the log behind her. Columbus stands at the right, and after a little while
sits beside her*).

                                    The deed that best
Proves each man's workmanship is what he is.
If God be the eternal, he who shows
Eternal perseverance falls not far
From fellow-craft with Him.

COLUMBUS.   You're like a myth
You're not inspired, but yet inspiring : not
Religion, but could make a man religious.

BEATRIX.   You speak in figures.

COLUMBUS.   We all live in them.

BEATRIX.   What then ?

COLUMBUS.   Why, they are beautiful.

BEATRIX.   And this
Gives life its beauty ?

COLUMBUS.   Ay, and interest.
For every time a spirit veiled in them

Reveals itself, why, it anticipates
The resurrection of the soul, not so?
And that brings heaven,

BEATRIX.   Then to reveal myself——

COLUMBUS.   Is very much in such a world as this—
When one owns so much that is worth revealing.

BEATRIX.   You jest.

COLUMBUS.   No; I'm in earnest.   When one needs
More strength of spirit, nothing save a spirit
Can ever give it.   You have given me yours.

BEATRIX.   'Tis true, I have.   Not seldom I have
        thought
That I could lose my soul to give it you.

COLUMBUS.   Thank God, a brother's love need not
        accept
The sacrifice.—But—should we linger here?
There's——

BEATRIX.   Well?

COLUMBUS.   Your relatives—

BEATRIX.   Of flesh, or soul?
I care but for the latter.   You——

COLUMBUS.   But yet
Their reasons are the world's too.   We're in Spain.
You are—

        *Enter—Right—from behind Columbus' tent—
        The* MOOR, *looks at* COLUMBUS *and* BEA-
        TRIX *then begins to draw away from the
        log the shawl that is beside and behind her.*

BEATRIX.   A virgin, yes, but were I *the*——

COLUMBUS. Do not say that——

BEATRIX. I could imagine times
That you would seem divine.

COLUMBUS. 'Tis very strange
How near together heaven and hell may be.

BEATRIX. 'Tis only earth and earthly thought that
make
It possible for sense to deem them two.
Throne God in hell, all heaven would burst the
gates
And dream of blessed rest, though every foot
Were sea'd upon a prostrate seething devil.

(*The shawl drawn by the* MOOR *disappears
from the log behind* BEATRIX. *Just as it
does so,* COLUMBUS *catches sight of it. The*
MOOR *starts back and wraps the shawl
about him.* COLUMBUS *rises.*)

COLUMBUS. What's that? (*to Beatrix who also rises.*)
Your shawl——

BEATRIX. Was taken?

COLUMBUS. Yes—drawn off.

BEATRIX. Some one was listening?

COLUMBUS. Yes—keep still.

(*Exit—Left Center—through the royal tent—
The* MOOR. COLUMBUS *sees him.*

I see
A form. It disappeared there in your tent.

BEATRIX. My shawl on?

COLUMBUS. Yes.

BEATRIX.   Why, all the ladies' tents—
    The queen's are reached through that.   I'll follow.
COLUMBUS.   No—
    A thief,—assassin, may be.   No, let me—
            (*Advancing toward the royal tent.*)
BEATRIX (*stopping him*).   Be thought a culprit?—
        never !
COLUMBUS (*handing her a dirk.*)   Then take this,
    And call me.   I will keep in hearing.—God !
    I cannot bear to let you go.
BEATRIX.   I must.

        Exit—Left Center—through the royal tent
            BEATRIX *with the dirk in hand.*

COLUMBUS.   How brave in her !   Yet what could
        one expect !
    How brave in her to let me know her love !
    And what unnatural, unmanned man am I,
    Who does not, will not dare, return it her !
    Strange mixture life is of the right and wrong !
    Should one be good, or kind? and which is
        which ?
    How much that seems to lead to both is but
    A ray that falls to form a pathway here
    From the rent forms of clouds beyond our reach
    That, while they let the light in, bring the storm !
VOICES (*from within the tent at Left Center*).
    Help, help !
COLUMBUS.   What's that ?

BEATRIX (*appearing at Left Center.*)

Columbus, come!—A Moor
Has killed the guard.

COLUMBUS. You rouse the camp.

(*Calling aloud*) A Moor!

Exit Left Center, COLUMBUS.

BEATRIX (*calling aloud*). A Moor!——

*Enter—Left Side Rear, Second and Front—*SANCHEZ
and SOLDIERS. BEATRIX *points to Left Center.*

In there!—He'll kill the queen.

*Exeunt—Left Center—*SANCHEZ *and* SOLDIERS.

VOICES (*from within the royal tent at Left Center*).
Ay, ay, take this and that.

Enter from Left Center, SANCHEZ, COLUMBUS *and*
SOLDIERS *dragging a dummy form of the* MOOR.

SANCHEZ. Here—drag him out!
There's no life left him. Humph! he's limp
enough
To make a rug of at the door.

Enter—Right Side Rear—other SOLDIERS, *the officer*
GUTIERREZ *and the* KING.

GUTIERREZ. The King.

(*All fall back. The* KING *looks at the* MOOR)

KING. Who is he?

SANCHEZ. An assassin—sought the queen—
Surprised the guard.

KING.   He did not reach her?

SANCHEZ.   No.

>   (*Pointing to* COLUMBUS.)

Well nigh!   He tracked him in.   We mastered
    him.

KING (*to* COLUMBUS).   Ay, ay!   Your name?

COLUMBUS.   Columbus.

KING (*to all.*)   We'll to rest.

>   (*To* COLUMBUS).

But you may come with me—Would see you
    further.

>   *Exeunt—Left   Center* KING,   GUTIERREZ,
>   COLUMBUS, SOLDIERS, BEATRIX.
>   *Exeunt at other entrances,* OMNES.

SCENE SECOND.—*Council Chamber in the Dominican
    Convent of St. Stephen at Salamanca.   Dark wood
    paneling in ceiling and walls.   A long table in the
    Rear with chairs behind it and at both ends.   En-
    trances at Right and Left sides.   Enter—Left—*
    ZALORA *and* FERNANDEZ.

FERNANDEZ.   You here?

ZALORA.   Oh yes.   One must obey the king.

FERNANDEZ.   He must suppose the times ahead
    are dark.

ZALORA.   How so?

FERNANDEZ.   In giving us this *pastime.*

ZALORA. We have our holy days and holidays.
I sometimes wonder which are holier.

FERNANDEZ. What, what! and you a priest?

ZALORA.   An old one—yes.
Like other earthly things, our lives move on
Half light, half shadow, and with me
The shadows came in youth.

FERNANDEZ.   Your brilliancy
Developed late, eh? like a winter's dawn—
Or lightning from a cloud. You're right, though,
     yes,
Life's like an air-ball: keep its youth-side in,
'Twill bulge out on its age-side. Say, does that
Make preachers, eh? sensational? You should
     know.

ZALORA. You think sensations are acquired?

*Enter—at Right—St. Angel and Perez and ex-
change greetings with Fernandez and Zalora.*

FERNANDEZ.   I know
A soul that squeals well, is a soul well squeezed.
Sensation is the step-son of depression.
You step on——

ZALORA.   Oh, go to!—that spoils the form.

ST. ANGEL. What form?

FERNANDEZ (*to* ST. ANGEL). Why, of a ball.
                    (*to* ZALORA) Not so?
                    (*to* ST. ANGEL) Tell why
A child's ball—say—and bishop are alike.

PEREZ (*laughing and pointing* to ZALORA).
  Because, like him, they're usually *round*?
ST. ANGEL.   And sometimes, though not always,
    holy, eh ?
ZALORA (*good-naturedly*).
  Don't point your wit with personality.
ST. ANGEL.   Oh never, never, when the person's
    blunt.
  But now the child's ball?
FERNANDEZ.   Why, the *bowl* is made
(*Brings his hands down as if ordaining, and also
          striking a blow*)
  By laying on of hands.
              (*All laugh.*)
      *Enter—Right—*MENDOZA *and* TALAVERA.
      *Enter—Left—*ARANA, FONSECA, BREVIESCA *and
          others.   All in, or entering, the hall ex-
          change greetings.*
TALAVERA (*to* FERNANDEZ).   What's this you're at ?
FERNANDEZ.   Our duty here—to deal with nonsense.
    You
Should know.   You sent for us.
ZALORA.   And why for me ?
  I'm not an expert on insanity.
FERNANDEZ (*to* ZALORA).   Oh no, you're on beyond
    an expert.
TALAVERA.   A present pert ?
FERNANDEZ.   Beyond that too.
ZALORA.   How so ?
FERNANDEZ.   Beyond an xpert is a y-z—pert.

ZALORA. That's low down in the alphabet of wit.

FERNANDEZ. I know —the *last* of it -just where
you *shoo* it.

FONSECA (*to* ARANA *in another part of the hall*).
But think.—the danger.

ARANA.   Oh, he'll never sail!

FONSECA. It's not in that, but in his theories.
You know they contradict the church.

ARANA.   If this
Be true—

FONSECA. It is. I say 'tis serious.

FERNANDEZ (*to* FONSECA). And what of that? I
say the best of physics
For seriousness is laughter. Where there's bile,
Well tickled throats will throw it up.

FONSECA.   To fool
With fools is feeding folly.

FERNANDEZ.   Feed a fool
On folly, and he grows so fat with it
That he protrudes, obtrudes, intrudes on all
'Till everybody sees the *dude* he is.

BREVIESCA. But he himself must see it.

FERNANDEZ.   If he's dull
And off his balance, balance him, ay, ay—
Get *even* with him—no great task for you!

TALAVERA. Come, come. We're making too much
light of this.

FERNANDEZ. What better can enlighten dullness,
pray,
Than *making light* of it?

BREVIESCA.   He's more than dull.
ST. ANGEL.   That must be proved.
ZALORA.   Aha! So you're his friend.
    Then tell us, if you can, just why we're here.
ST. ANGEL.   Why, to report about Columbus.
FERNANDEZ.   Humph!
    About him's good.   How far about him, pray?
ST. ANGEL.   The truth.
FERNANDEZ.   What, what?   We're not to exercise
    Our minds?—let them revolve about, and then
    Evolve——
FONSECA.   Oh, cease your jesting!

> *All begin to take places around the table, though
> not yet to sit.* TALAVERA *goes to the central
> seat behind it,* MENDOZA *to his right, and
> ST. ANGEL and* PEREZ *to the right of* MEN-
> DOZA.   FONSECA, BREVIESCA, ARANA,
> ZALORA *and* FERNANDEZ *are at* TALA-
> VERA'S *Left.   Others sit where there are
> places.*

FERNANDEZ.   I'm in earnest.
    We're a committee sitting on Columbus.
    An old hen, even, doing this, I say,
    Would hatch out something.   We're committee-
        men.
    Men are creative.   All things else are creatures.
    Am I to act the man, or prate the parrot?
FONSECA.   We'll show you.
ST. ANGEL (*to* PEREZ).   Ay, they'll show us, as I think,

Birds of *another's feather*—birds of *prey.*
PEREZ. They follow their profession then.
ST. ANGEL. In that—
    And making mortals humble. Give one aught
    To plume himself on, he'll not go unplucked.
    But there's the victim.
                *Enter—Right—*COLUMBUS.
TALAVERA (*to those in the chamber*).
                        Gentlemen, Columbus.
            (*To* COLUMBUS *and all.*)
I think you've met before.
            (COLUMBUS *and all exchange greetings.*)
                        We all are here.
    We'll sit, not so?
            The others sit. TALAVERA *motions to*
            COLUMBUS *to do the same, which he does at*
            the extreme Right.
                    Where thought appeals to thought,
    The only sovereign is the wisest word,
    Which sometimes is the last one. Even if first,
    'Tis always of the spirit, and needs not
    Accoutrements and courtesies of form
    To prove its prestige. We can waive them, then,
    And let the spirit prompt us as it may.
            (*Turning to* COLUMBUS.)
    'Tis said you wish to have a fleet and men,
    And outfit, too, involving much expense.
    What reasons have you?
COLUMBUS. To extend the sway
    5

Of Spain and Christianity in lands
Where now they are not known.

TALAVERA.   That wish is ours.
What proof have you, though, that these lands
    exist?

COLUMBUS.   Reports of mariners—authority—
The nature of the world.

TALAVERA.   Do these off-set
The dangers?

COLUMBUS.   Which ones?

ARANA.   Like the boiling waves
Of Africa, and giants on the shores.

COLUMBUS.   Mere fables, all!   Why, I myself have
    sailed
To Guinea, past where these were said to be,
And have you never heard of Eudoxus
Of Cyzicus, who left Arabia
And reached Gibraltar! how too from Gibraltar
The Carthaginian Hanno, sailing back,
Came to Arabia?

FONSECA.   All pagan lies!

COLUMBUS.   A statement that confutes a general
    faith
At risk of reputation: yet meantime
Confirms our natural reasoning, seldom lies.
Who would have said this, had it not been true?
Yet that it should be, what more natural?

ZALORA.   But sailing east is not the same as west.

COLUMBUS.   Enough is known to warrant even that.

FERNANDEZ.   St. Brandan and the seven cities, yes !
     But then they've always melted into clouds
     To those who've sought them.
COLUMBUS.   There are many more.
MENDOZA.   Atlantis, eh ?
COLUMBUS.   Yes, and Antilla too,
     Well known to Carthage, Aristotle says.
     And many a modern vessel has been driven
     Where shores have been descried by accident
     And other signs of ——
FONSECA.   Desert islands.
COLUMBUS.   No,
     Vicenti, twenty score of leagues beyond
     The Cape St. Vincent, came on floating wood
     Carved by men's hands.
ZALORA.   Ay, from some other ship.
COLUMBUS.   Then lost in many places.   Wood
          carved thus
     Was found by my own brother Correo,
     And plants and trees too drift thus from the west.
FONSECA.   Washed there, washed back.
COLUMBUS.   No, different in kind
     From any in the East.   They've found besides
     Two men's forms cast upon the isle of Flores,
     With features not at all like men known here.
ARANA.   And what of that ?
COLUMBUS.   The men—not only they—
     The trees, the plants, are like in kind to those
     Described by Polo and by Mandeville.

As found in those great lands of Gengis Khan
And Prester John, far in the Indies.
ARANA.   But
   They're east, not west.
COLUMBUS.   Just so, both east and west.
FERNANDEZ.   What's that?
BREVIESCA (*to* FERNANDEZ).   You see——
COLUMBUS.   This seems a contradiction.
   It would not, did you think the world were round.
FONSECA (*laughing*).   No, never, no!
ARANA.   He's right, ha, ha!
ZALORA (*to* COLUMBUS *sarcastically*).   You're right.
COLUMBUS.   There is authority for thinking this.
ARANA.   For fancying it, yes: or anything.
COLUMBUS.   But Aristotle, Seneca and Pliny
   Say one can sail from Cadiz to the Indies.
TALAVERA.   Yet wait.   Besides this, is it not a fact
   That they too calculated three years' time,—
   Enough to starve a ship's crew ten times over——
   Before her cruise could compass it?
COLUMBUS.   Some did;
   Yet, judging by the globe of Ptolemy,
   Compared with one Marinus made, of Tyre,
   There's but a third of it that's unexplored,—
   Eight hours of twenty-four.   You measure this.
   It can't be more than seven hundred leagues.
FONSECA.   You measure it?—The whole thing's
        merely fancy.
ARANA.   There's not a ray of reason in it.

FONSECA.   No.

ARANA (*to* COLUMBUS). And, granting earth's a
    globe—What, then, forsooth?—
  Could sail around it, without tumbling off?

FONSECA (*to* ZALORA). Ay, or without the water's
    tumbling off?

ARANA.   Same thing!

FERNANDEZ (*good-naturedly to Columbus*).
               I think that you must be the man
  I've heard of often, though I've never seen him,
  Who wants to turn the whole world upside-
    down——

FONSECA.   Where roots of trees bear leaves, and
    rain spurts up.

BREVIESCA.   He'll be at home there.—better let him
    go!
  His own head's upside down already.

FERNANDEZ.   You wait now. This is science. They
    examined
  The feet of men they found at Flores: not so?

ZALORA.   They did?

FERNANDEZ.   Oh yes! and found them shaped like
    spider's,
  Made to walk up like this.
           (*Gesturing with his hands.*)

BREVIESCA.   I've seen that kind
  Clawed on a pictured devil.

FONSECA.   If he sail,
  He'll see them soon enough upon a real one.

TALAVERA. Oh, now!

FONSECA.   I mean it : ay, I speak the truth.
  The holy father, St. Augustine, shows it :
  Men formed like this—to walk thus upside-
      down—
  Could not be sons of Adam.   Did they live,
  'Twould overthrow our whole historic base
  Of Christian faith.

ARANA.   Just so!

FONSECA.   To argue it
  At all, grant it conceivable—what's that
  But heresy?

ZALORA.   Hear, hear!

ARANA.   You're right

BREVIESCA.   Ay, ay.

COLUMBUS. But are you sure these men are not
      like us?

FONSECA. You'll have to practice many years be-
      fore
  You'll walk with your heels up.

COLUMBUS.   But there, as here,
  The earth may seem to be below one.

ARANA.   Ah!
  We grant to fancy, man, a certain flight.
  We've witnessed one to-day.   But do you dream
  It's wings could turn us all to flies
  Without our knowing it ?

COLUMBUS.   There may be laws
  Of nature past our understanding.

BREVIESCA.   Yes.
  He means that when we lose our understanding—
  He's had experience of that—why then——
TALAVERA. Come, no more nonsense, gentlemen.
ZALORA (*rising*).   No more?
  Time to adjourn then, eh? There's nothing else
  Before the house.
COLUMBUS (*rising to address* ZALORA).
                          In such a case as this,
  In which none know the truth——
FONSECA (*rising*).   Your pardon, but
  The Scriptures say: "He stretcheth out the
      heavens "—
  How?—like a ball?—No, no; but "like a tent."
  You dare throw doubt upon the word of Him
  Who framed creation?
COLUMBUS.   What you quote is but
A figure.
FONSECA.   Fiction?
COLUMBUS.   Figure—not the same.
BREVIESCA. Accuse of figuring—Him who knows
      the end
  From the beginning—all the sum at once?
  He does not figure up. He counts the whole.
TALAVERA (*to* BREVIESCA). Oh, you mistake his
      meaning!
BREVIESCA (*looking around incredulously*). What?
FERNANDEZ (*to* BREVIESCA).   Yes, yes.
COLUMBUS (*paying no attention to* BREVIESCA).

Were one upon the other side the globe,
The heavens might seem as like a tent as here.

FONSECA. They only might? The Scriptures say
they do.
You make them doubtful?

BREVIESCA.   Heretic!

ARANA.   Too true!

COLUMBUS. My one desire, the purpose of my life
Is to become an earthly instrument
Through which the Scriptures may become fulfilled,
That all the ends of earth—they are ends now—
Be brought together with one Lord and God.

FONSECA. What good would this do, if His word
were false?

COLUMBUS (*in surprise*). You think I deem it so?

FONSECA.   We've heard you term
Its affirmations figures, argue down—
And that with pagan proofs—the fathers. Truth
Can never change.

COLUMBUS.   We can.

FONSECA.   And change it?

COLUMBUS.   Change
Its bearings for us. Truth is of the heaven:
The mind regarding it is of the earth.
The one is infinite, the other finite:
The one expressed in light itself, the other
In forms that but reflect light; and the truth,
Made such but by reflection, cannot flash
An equal ray to every view-point.

SEVERAL. Oh!

COLUMBUS. Give blind men sight. At first their
new-viewed sun

  Will stand still in the heaven. But give them
time,

  'Twill set and rise. Then give them space, as
well,

  Lift them a thousand miles above the soil,

  It may do neither.

ARANA. Dangerous doctrine that!

FONSECA (*to* COLUMBUS). There's no truth then?

COLUMBUS. There's truth enough for all.

  But truth expressed is coin to use, not hoard.

  For when it bears the stamp of times too old,

  It loses current value.

FONSECA. Hear that! hear!

  Why, that blasphemes tradition!

BREVIESCA. Just as if

  Antiquity itself did not prove truth!

COLUMBUS. The moonlight guides us, if we have
no sun.

  But forms that loom at midnight lie to those

  Who know them in the day: and in the day

  No judgment of the distance can be true

  Except to him who pushes on to reach it.

FONSECA. Hold! Hold! Enough of this! There
is a law

  That ought to be enforced here.

ARANA. We shall see!

COLUMBUS. The world will see in time that I am
      right.
   No theory spun for concepts immature
   Can ever fit their full maturity.
            Enter—Right—an ATTENDANT.
TALAVERA (*rising*). A moment, gentlemen.
            (*To* ATTENDANT.)
                                    What is it ?
ATTENDANT.   Here's
   The royal courier.
TALAVERA.   Ah, has come so soon ?
            (*To all.*)
   Then for to-day our conference must end.
            (*All who are sitting rise.*)
COLUMBUS (*to* TALAVERA).
   And I withdraw ?
TALAVERA (*bowing in assent and adieu to* COLUMBUS).
            We thank you for your candor.
(COLUMBUS *bows to all the council, and the council to*
            him.)
*Exeunt—Right—*COLUMBUS *and* ATTENDANT, *show-*
            ing him out.
FONSECA (*moving with others toward the Left*).
   But we must see we have no more of it.
FERNANDEZ (*to* ZALORA, TALAVERA *and* MENDOZA,
      who are walking behind FONSECA, ARANA,
      BREVIESCA *and others*).
   A spark in hayloft ! bull in porcelain !
   We'll have the whole church crackling round us yet.

Exeunt — Left — FONSECA, ARANA, BREVIESCA *and others.*

MENDOZA (*to* FERNANDEZ).
  But racy as a bull fight?

FERNANDEZ.   In the which
  The bull did some tall tossing.

Exeunt—Left—First MENDOZA, *then* ZALORA, TALA-
VERA *and* FERNANDEZ.

PEREZ (*to* ST. ANGEL).   Did you hear? —
  Strange words for him.

ST. ANGEL.   Oh, no ! I've always found
  The light mind is the bright mind. Wit and wits
  Are twins ; when one is absent, both are lacking.
      *Exeunt—Right—*ST. ANGEL *and all others.*

SCENE THIRD.—*Exterior of the Convent of La Rabida,
near the little seaport of Palos, in Andalusia, in
Spain. Backing, a wall, behind which are hills,
trees, and a distant sea-view. At the right, a gateway
opening into the Convent. At the left, trees, etc.
Entrances at Right Side Rear, behind the Convent;
Right Side, further forward, through a gateway
opening into the Convent; Left Side Rear and
Front through trees.*

*Enter—Right Side Rear—*BEATRIX *and* DIEGO *in
out-door costumes.*

BEATRIX.   I could not keep him back.

DIEGO.   You tried to block
His pathway, eh? but he looked over you—
Beyond you?

BEATRIX.   Humph! poor treatment from a friend!

DIEGO.   You wished to fill his whole horizon then?

BEATRIX.   Why—in a friend——

DIEGO.   'Tis easy enough to do:
Make friends of little souls: they're common.

BEATRIX (*offended*).   What?

DIEGO.   A spirit's measure is its outlook.   Find
A man horizoned by a world of worlds,
And all in all and always, he's a son
Of God.   He's here to do his Father's work;
And you must join in it, or not join him.

BEATRIX.   Why should he go to France?—no sailors
there.

DIEGO.   A spirit conscious of a higher mission
Is always on the wing.

BEATRIX.   You know our king
Gave weight to his suggestions, promised ships?

DIEGO.   But would not place my brother in command.

BEATRIX.   'Twas safer so.

DIEGO.   For whom?

BEATRIX.   Columbus.

DIEGO.   What?
You talked of his own safety to my brother?

BEATRIX.   Why, he had done his duty, sown his seed;
Then why not leave the rest to Providence?

DIEGO.   Fling seed to seas, or hope 'twill root in
         winds ;
But do not trust your thoughts to Providence.
Their soil is in humanity, nor there
Spring, grow, or ripen without husbandry.
BEATRIX.   He's talked and argued——
DIEGO.   Oh, to talk the truth
Is easy as to breathe.   To live the truth.
And, mailed in its pure radiance, burn to black
The shade its white heat touches, needs a strength
To suffer hatred and inspire to love,
Half hell's, half heaven's, and wholly Christ's.
BEATRIX.   And yet
If others sail——
DIEGO.   The goal is so far off,
And so unseen, that all but faith will fail ;
And this they lack.
BEATRIX.   But yet, you told him, too,
You thought 'twas vain to leave here.
DIEGO.   Feared 'twas vain.
But you, you urged him to submit, not sail,
Nor push his claims upon the king.
BEATRIX.   Of course.
DIEGO.   Poor, lonely man !
BEATRIX.   His own fault—would not have
A soul go with him.
DIEGO.   Why should he ?   To minds
In which the spirit so subdues the sense,
A lack of sympathy itself is absence.

BEATRIX.   But you will join him?

DIEGO.   Like a faithful slave
Whom word, not thought, commands.

BEATRIX.   Why should not I?

DIEGO.   You're better off at home than with a man
With no home either for himself or you.
He's often told you that.

BEATRIX.   A home's a state,
Not place.

DIEGO.   A state of happiness, and that
He knows he could not give you.

BEATRIX.   Do you think
We'll really see him here?

DIEGO.   Why, yes, I think
They'll find him; and, if so, they'll bring him back.
He can't oppose a meeting with the queen.

BEATRIX.   You say she lunches with the monks to-
day?

DIEGO.   I heard so, yes—
              (*Pointing toward Left Side Rear.*)
                    And look she's coming now.

BEATRIX.   I have some faith in her.

DIEGO.   Faith always waits
On perfect womanhood.   Show men a form
Whose symmetry of outward nature frames
A symmetry of soul, whose pure-hued face
Complexions pureness of the character,
Whose clear sweet accents outlet clear, sweet
thought,

Whose burning eyes flash flame from kindled
    love,
And all whose yielding gracefulness of mien
But fitly robes all gracious sympathy,—
Ay, find a soul whose beauty of the shield
But keeps more bright the blade of brain because
Of what seems merely ornament,—to her
All men must yield a spirit's loyalty.
She's fairy-goddess of the world of fact,
Dream-sister of the brotherhood of deeds,
An angel minister as well as queen,
Whom all the splendor of high station lifts
But like the sun that it may light us all.

Enter—Left Side Rear—the QUEEN *and* ATTENDANTS,
    among them ST. ANGEL.

    *Enter—at the same time—at Right Side
    through the convent's gateway,* MONKS,
    among them PEREZ, *behind them* SANCHEZ
    and COLUMBUS.

PEREZ (*to the* QUEEN *to whom all do reverence*).
  We feel much honored by your presence
QUEEN.   Nay,
  You are the ministers of higher power.
  The honor comes to me.
BEATRIX (*to* DIEGO *in the rear*).
                    There is Columbus.
DIEGO. They've found him then.
BEATRIX.   I wonder what he'll say.

PEREZ.   Your majesty, your couriers have re-
    turned.
    They found Columbus.
QUEEN.   Yes? and where?
PEREZ.   Far up
    The mountains, just this side the boundary.
QUEEN.   Alone?
PEREZ   Alone.
                    (*introducing* COLUMBUS) Columbus.
                    (COLUMBUS *salutes the* QUEEN.)
QUEEN (*to* COLUMBUS).   As I hoped
    And you were leaving us?
COLUMBUS.   I was.
QUEEN.   Why so?
COLUMBUS.   I have an aim in life.

            (BEATRIX, *in her gestures towards* DIEGO, *to
                which she tries to attract the attention of*
                COLUMBUS, *expresses disapproval of his
                answers which follow here.*)

QUEEN.   I thought the king
    Had promised ships.
COLUMBUS.   He had.
QUEEN.   And officers.
COLUMBUS.   Not those for such an undertaking.
QUEEN.   You
    Can go with them.
COLUMBUS.   Your pardon, but—I beg—
    Excuse me.

QUEEN. Why?

COLUMBUS. I have no time to waste.

QUEEN. To waste?

COLUMBUS. 'Tis eighteen years since I began
  To urge this project. I'm no longer young.

QUEEN. Why, ships and men, and you to sail
  with them!—

COLUMBUS. Sail off, sail back—I have no time to
  waste.

QUEEN. You think they would not persevere?

COLUMBUS. The goal
  Is not of their discerning.—Why should they
  Be thought the ones to bring it to the light?

QUEEN. But they——

COLUMBUS. To them 'tis but a madman's whim,
  A thing to flout. To me the one conception
  Of all that is most rational and holy.
  Which, then, would give his life that it might
  live?

QUEEN. Why, we had hopes that none would need
  do that.

COLUMBUS. And hopes well based; yet any man
  who sails
  Across that unknown sea must show far more
  Than enterprise, experience, caution, skill,
  Knowledge of sail and compass, wind and star.
  His soul must be embarked upon the voyage
  With aims outreaching all that but concern
  The narrow limits of this earthly life.

QUEEN. How few such men! Where would you
    find your crew?

COLUMBUS. Wherever mind is subject to ideas.

QUEEN. And where is that?—You judge men by
    yourself.

COLUMBUS. I would not dare to boast such differ-
    ence,

  Or so humiliate my humanity,

  As to presume it possible that aims

  Inspiring my own soul, if rightly urged,

  Would not inspire, too, many another.

QUEEN.   Yes,

  I can believe it, with yourself to urge them.

  And were you given command, would you collect

  A crew and sail with them?

COLUMBUS.   No man can reach

  A problem's right solution, if he fail

  To calculate aright the means.

QUEEN.   Of course—

  And that——

COLUMBUS. Has not been done in this case.

QUEEN.   No?

  What more would you require?

COLUMBUS.   Ten times the sum

  That has been promised.

QUEEN.   'Tis impossible.

  There's not that in the treasury.

COLUMBUS.   I would give

  The whole I have—both property and life.

SANCHEZ.   And I.

QUEEN.   You would?—you're rich.

SANCHEZ.   I would.

DIEGO (*coming forward and bowing before the* QUEEN).
                                        And I,

   Though I have nothing—only what you see.

ST. ANGEL.   Your Majesty, with men like these,
      prepared

   To root their very spirits out from earth,

   That they may thus transplant them where the
      world

   Will reap a richer fruitage, what were Spain,

   Were she to grudge a void from which were
      scraped

   A paltry heap of gold! 'Twere all too mean

   To pedestal aright the lasting fame

   That would be hers, did they attain their end.

QUEEN.   'Tis true, and yet the royal treasury——

ST. ANGEL.   Are there no treasures elsewhere than
     in that?

QUEEN (*hesitating a moment*).

   There are. If I be queen, let me be queen

   Of Spanish spirit as of Spanish soil.

   I will—there is a treasure.—What to Spain

   Are her most precious treasures, which most deck

   The crown that they surround, and keep it bright?

   Mere jewels, think you?—Nay, not these, but men.

   And if I give the one to gain the other, who

   Could strike a better bargain? Ay, I will—

I pledge you the crown jewels of Castile.
I pledge you the commandership.   Enough !
Columbus, you shall go.

COLUMBUS (*falling on his knees before her*).

God bless the queen.

(*The others fall on their knees beside* COLUMBUS.)

(CURTAIN.)

End of Act Second.

ACT THIRD.

SCENE FIRST.—*A street in Palos de Moguer, in Andalusia. Backing, a distant harbor, with ships. At the Right, a porch before the house of* BEATRIX. *At the Left, other houses. Entrances, Right Side Rear, behind the house of* BEATRIX; *Right Side Second, through a door opening from this house onto the porch in front of it; Right Side Front, through the street in front of this house; Left Side Rear and Front, through streets.*

(*The curtain rising discloses* COLUMBUS *and* BEATRIX, *standing on or near the porch.*)

COLUMBUS. Now I must off, and see the ships. You know
I've been a week away.

BEATRIX.   You met the queen?

COLUMBUS. And king, and got their last instructions.

BEATRIX.   Oh,
I cannot bear to have you sail !

COLUMBUS.   Nor I
To leave you.

BEATRIX.   Yet——

COLUMBUS.   I must.

BEATRIX.   Oh, yes, you must!

COLUMBUS. Our lives are finite, but the aims of
    life
  Are infinite, and crowd on every side.
  Whate'er we strive to reach, in thought, in
      deed,
  At last, some one aim surely tips the balance;
  As it has weight, the others are thrown up.

BEATRIX. No matter who goes with them?

COLUMBUS.   I had hoped,
  Now that my project seems, at last, afloat,
  That your soul would be buoyant as is mine.

BEATRIX. Yes, yes, but yet can it be worth the
      price?

COLUMBUS. I know your meaning.—loss of life,
      perhaps,
  And all for which some prize life,—ease and love.
  I've told you so before, it is worth this,
  And others go with me who think the same.

BEATRIX. Some call them fools.

COLUMBUS.   Some?—where?

BEATRIX.   In all the streets.

COLUMBUS. Here?

BEATRIX.   Yes.

COLUMBUS.   They are fools, if this life be all;
  And fools, as well, if they but claim 'tis all.
  For, risking dangers thick as mid-sea-mist
  In war, in wave, men's deeds outdo their words,

And prove they serve a grander sovereignty.
Whose realms outreach all death-lines.

BEATRIX.   Is it these
  You seek in that cloud-compassed, storm-set sea?
  Ah, how can I put it before your life?—
  Or, how can you?

COLUMBUS.   I've said I did not know.
  What moves me seems beyond all conscious
      thought
  'Tis like the lure that leads the summer bird
  Southward when comes the winter. 'Tis enough,
  It is my destiny. I weigh it well,
  And find it rational; yet why I first
  Conceived it as I do, I cannot tell.

              *Enter—Left Side Rear—*DIEGO.

DIEGO (*to himself, as he looks at Beatrix*). Like all
      the other women in the town,
  She's leagued to keep him back, eh? Oh, 'tis not
  In nature that a man obey a woman.
  And human ways, when not in nature, bode
  Th' inhuman somewhere. Humph! I'll let him
      know
  That none can turn to *she* the pronoun *he*
  Without an *s* that puts a hiss before it.
              (*To* COLUMBUS.)
  My brother?

COLUMBUS (*to* DIEGO). Ay?

DIEGO. There's business (DIEGO *and* BEATRIX *bow
      to each other*).

COLUMBUS.   I know it—(*to* BEATRIX),
    I'll find you later.   You'll excuse me now.

Exit—Right Side Second—into her house, BEATRIX.

DIEGO. You should have come before.   That
    woman's gowns
    Are always clinging to you—look as if
    She thought to make a woman of yourself.
    Confound their sex !
COLUMBUS. Not all now ! There are some——
DIEGO. Some men too : but in all of Spain, not six
    To man your vessels of their own free will.
    Why not ?—Because not fit to go with you.
    How many women, think you, fit for it ?
COLUMBUS. Don't be so hard upon them.
DIEGO.   No, they're soft,
    As soft as cats, and mew, too, ay and scratch.
    I've seen their blisters ! ay, I've seen a man
    Whose very soul had been scratched out by one.
COLUMBUS. You talk as if you feared for me.
DIEGO.   I fear
    For all the expedition.   You've not heard
    The news.
COLUMBUS. What is it ?
DIEGO.   Everything that's bad.
COLUMBUS. The ships are——
DIEGO.   Floating.   You may thank the guards.
    The crews have all deserted.
COLUMBUS.   What ?

DIEGO.   As if
  The howlings of their wives and mothers here
  About their ears, could bring them less of hell
  Than howlings of the wind upon the sea!
COLUMBUS.   The women have persuaded them to
      break
  Their word with us?
DIEGO.   Why, yes.   Who else would, eh?
  What woman ever cared about her word—
  Her own word or her husband's?   Bless her jaws!
  So many more words there, she doesn't need it.
COLUMBUS.   Oh, waive the women!   Is it true the
      crew
  Have all deserted?
DIEGO.   Almost all.
COLUMBUS.   But yet
  The government— —
DIEGO.   Of course, they've sent around
  Arresting some, imprisoning others.   Oh,
  You'll have enough of them!   They've found a
      source
  That's inexhaustible.
COLUMBUS.   What's that?
DIEGO.   The jail.
  Which, like an Arab-shirt turned inside out,
  Will shake its lice upon you.
COLUMBUS.   That, at least,
  Will give us men.
DIEGO.   If you can call them men,

These creatures, whom a life-long fear of day
Has trained to crawl through nights of treachery;—
Sneaks, too irresolute and indolent
To push by honest means to worthy ends.
But I would trust in waves adrift for hell
As soon as helms in hands of criminals.
What can you ever do with such as these
When three months out at sea ?

COLUMBUS.   I must depend
Upon my officers.

DIEGO.   You're sure of them ?
You never know a coward till he's cowed
By gusts that can out-wind his self-conceit ;
And garbs they guise in, never cloud the air
In time for us to brace the fence they fell.
I wish that I were going with you.

COLUMBUS.   No :
We've talked that over.   One should stay behind
To guard our interests here.

*Enter—Left Side Rear—*GUTIERREZ.

DIEGO.   He's needed, too,
Far more than you could guess.   This officer
Will tell you.   He's the one has been in charge.

GUTIERREZ (*exchanging salute with* COLUMBUS).
We're glad to see you back, sir.

COLUMBUS.   Thanks.
The ships are safe and ready ?

GUTIERREZ.   Guarded, sir,

All night, all day. Some men here took an oath,
Perhaps you know, to scuttle them.
COLUMBUS.   They did?
I'm glad they've not succeeded.
GUTIERREZ.   No, of course.
We always guard a ship that's been impressed
For royal services, like treasure. Still
They came within an inch of it.
COLUMBUS.   How so?
GUTIERREZ. We thought that Breviesca was your
    friend.
COLUMBUS. Quite otherwise, I fear.
GUTIERREZ.   You're right, but yet,
As agent of Fonseca, Bishop of——
COLUMBUS. Oh, worse and worse! The bishop, I
    believe,
Would be assured that only truth had triumphed,
If I and all the crew were drowned.
GUTIERREZ.   Ah, so?
Well, they have tried it.
COLUMBUS.   What?
GUTIERREZ.   To have you drowned.
COLUMBUS. You mean?——
GUTIERREZ.   Tried to corrupt the calkers.
COLUMBUS.   No!——
You're sure of that?
GUTIERREZ.   'Twas overheard.
COLUMBUS.   Good God!——
This man Breviesca?

GUTIERREZ.   Yes, 'twas he.
COLUMBUS.   And you?——
GUTIERREZ.   We turned the calkers off; and had a
    task
  Impressing others.   When 'twas done, we put
  A soldier back of every one to calk
  His pores with steel unless he calked the ships'.
COLUMBUS.   And now they're ready?
GUTIERREZ.   Will be, by to-night.
COLUMBUS.   We'll sail to-morrow, then.
GUTIERREZ.   Meantime, perhaps—
  You'll pardon me—you'll hold yourself unseen?
COLUMBUS.   Why so?
GUTIERREZ.   To save a conflict with the mob.
COLUMBUS.   You mean that——
GUTIERREZ.   They might keep you here by force;
  Or sacrifice your life, and readily,
  To save their friends.   They deem all these are
    doomed.
DIEGO.   Why, very victims burning at the stake
  Could never cause a cloud more black than seems
  To hang above the town to-day.
COLUMBUS (*to* GUTIERREZ).   I see,
  Your hint's of value.   I'll be with you soon.

  *Exit—Left Side Rear—*GUTIERREZ, *after saluting.*
      COLUMBUS *continues to* DIEGO.

  So so!   You note what influenced Beatrix.
DIEGO.   Of course.   A man but in his public thought

Thermometers the public sentiment.
A woman does it in her private thought ;
And woe to lovers who dare say their say
Without a little clique that, echoing it,
Can make it seem, at least, a little public.
COLUMBUS.   But you can't blame her—
DIEGO.   Trend the fashion ?   No.
You flaunt the flag of fashion in a crowd
And, in the bee-line of their rush to tail
Its leading, one could pick the women out
Without **their** having skirts on.
COLUMBUS.   I must send
To Pinzon.   He expects me at his house.
DIEGO.   Yes, I'll go.
COLUMBUS.   Thanks, and say that I must wait,
And meet him at the ships.   See Perez too,
And tell him that we sail at dawn, and wish
The sacrament.   I know he'll come.   We'll use
The little chapel that's beside the dock.
DIEGO.   I will.

               *Exit—Right Side Front—*DIEGO.
COLUMBUS (*to himself*).   Now I'll go this way—
(*looking toward the left, then at the house of* BEATRIX)
                         Though I ought
To say a word more here.   When courtesy
And caution balance in the scales, the heart
Is kinder than the head, if not more wise.
*Enter—Right Side Rear—*BREVIESCA, PINTOR, *and*
                    ROLDAN.

BREVIESCA (*stepping between* COLUMBUS *and the house
        of* BEATRIX).
    Columbus ?
COLUMBUS.   Breviesca !
BREVIESCA.   Yes, I wish
    To speak to you.
COLUMBUS.   You have your wish.
BREVIESCA.   I bring
    An invitation from the bishop.
COLUMBUS.   Which—
    Fonseca ?
BREVIESCA.   Yes.
COLUMBUS.   And where is he ?
BREVIESCA.   Why, at
    The monastery.
COLUMBUS.   On the other side
    The town, not so ?—and what's his object ?
BREVIESCA.   Oh !—
    About the mission that the church has planned.
COLUMBUS.   These matters have been all arranged.
BREVIESCA.   But he
    Would see you.
COLUMBUS.   He can see me at my ship.
BREVIESCA.   He's full of work.
COLUMBUS.   Then give him my regrets.
BREVIESCA.   But he demands your presence.
COLUMBUS.   No ; I'm not
    Within his jurisdiction.
ROLDAN.   Ho ! hear that.

PINTOR. **He's** right, though! He's no Spaniard;
no—a dog
Of Genoa—no Christian—a Chris-*chin*.

COLUMBUS. I've work the queen has ordered. I
must do it.

BREVIESCA (*laughing and pointing to the house of*
BEATRIX).
Yes, yes, the *queen of hearts.*

PINTOR. A pretty *game!*
She's taken by a *knave.*

COLUMBUS. It might be well
To imitate the mien of gentlemen.

BREVIESCA. And you of Christians, and obey the
bishop.

COLUMBUS. I've given you my answer.

PINTOR. Frightened eh? —
Aha!—would get behind the soldiers there.
(*Pointing toward the ships and harbor at the Left*).

COLUMBUS. A man who lives for others, not for
self,
Has little fear for self; yet care for them
May give him caution. I've the best of reasons
For keeping eyes upon the ships.

PINTOR (*sarcastically and looking significantly at*
BREVIESCA *and* ROLDAN).
Oh, yes!

BREVIESCA (*approaching* COLUMBUS *and laying his
hand on him*).
Say, will you go with me?—I think you will.

COLUMBUS (*knocking* BREVIESCA *down*).

    Yes, yes, when I'm down there with you, I will.

*Enter—Left Side—*GUTIERREZ *with two* SOLDIERS.

*Enter—Right Side Front—*DIEGO.

*Exit—Right Side Rear—*PINTOR *and* ROLDAN.

DIEGO. What is it?

COLUMBUS.   Why, I'm practicing, you see—
    On criminals.—That man there set a trap.
    But it takes two to make a trap work.   He,
    He was a genius, this man, played both rôles.
    He set it and was caught in it.

*Exit—Right Side Rear—*BREVIESCA, *crawling anxiously away.*

DIEGO *and* GUTIERREZ *start to follow and arrest him.*
COLUMBUS *motions them back with his hand.*

                      No no!

DIEGO. And you, my brother?   Such a patient
    man?

COLUMBUS. Oh, patient!   When a fire's been
    smouldering
    For eighteen years, don't blame it's blazing out.
    Thank God it did not wholly blast the fool
    Who sought to stir it—thought it had no life.
    The villain! if I only could be sure
    He would be better for the punishment!

DIEGO. You go now to the ships?

COLUMBUS.   Yes, very soon.

GUTIERREZ. Shall I go with you?

COLUMBUS (*ascending the porch of the house of*
BEATRIX). Wait here if you choose.

Not yet, I think, of all men living, I,
By this time, should have learned to go alone.

*Exit—Right Side Front—*DIEGO.

*Exit—Right Side—through the porch—*COLUMBUS.

GUTIERREZ *motions to the soldiers as if setting a guard
about the house of* BEATRIX.

Exit—Right Side Front—one SOLDIER.

Exeunt—Right Side Rear—other SOLDIER *and* GUTI-
ERREZ.

SCENE SECOND—*The deck of the ship of*
COLUMBUS. *Backing, sky and sea: at
first, invisible, because it is night; later
visible, as at sunrise; and, if thought best,
representing, in a panorama, a gradual
approach of the ships to shore, the scenery
moving from Right to Left. At the right
is the bow of the ship. At the left, a
cabin with a deck above it, on which* SAILORS
*can stand. There are also masts, sails,
and various arrangements which will
readily suggest themselves, a compass,
ropes, railings, etc.*

*Entrances—Left Side Rear—and—Left Side
Front—on each side of the cabin:—Left
Side Second—into the cabin, as well as just*

*above the cabin on to the upper deck.
Right Center—through a hatchway into
the ship's hold.*

ROLDAN *appears at the bow of the ship,* ESCOBAR
near him, and PINTOR *nearer the cabin.
Other* SAILORS *also are present.*

ROLDAN (*looking off through the dark*).   I'm sick of
this.

PINTOR.   And so am I.

ESCOBAR.   You wait.
Another storm will make you sicker still.

PINTOR.   If it would only sicken him.

ROLDAN.   Make him
Throw up, eh?
                    Yes, throw up the voyage.

ESCOBAR.   Oh,
"Twill come in time.   But when it comes, my
lad,
The ship will throw up us too.

PINTOR.   I know now
How fish feel when they see the water boil,
Just when we drop them in alive.

ESCOBAR.   They're not
More out their element than we are here,
With these few planks between ourselves and
hell.

PINTOR.   Nor any more sure, either, to be cooked.

ROLDAN.   What means it all ?—those weeks without
a stir

Amid the waves, and then those heavy swells
Without a stir amid the winds?

ESCOBAR.   What means it?—
Why, like enough we're getting near the place
Where all the waters pour down hill.

ROLDAN.   What's that?—
The edge?

ESCOBAR. Why not?—In streams you always find
Smooth, rapid water, waves, and then the plunge.

ROLDAN. It's quiet now.

ESCOBAR.   So is a cataract
Just where it nears the brink.

ROLDAN.   'Tis horrible!
You don't believe——-

ESCOBAR.   There must have been some cause,
What was it? There was not a wind.

PINTOR.   And when
There was, ten times to one 'twas blowing west.
That's not a wind will ever blow us home.

ESCOBAR. And what wind think you will, or can?

ROLDAN.   Or can?

ESCOBAR. Humph! let him keep on here, a day or
    two,
These floating weeds will hold us like a vise.

ROLDAN. He says they're signs of land.

ESCOBAR.   Oh, yes, of land!—
That fatal land afloat in fatal seas
Entrapping in their meshes all the ships
That dare to venture near.

ROLDAN (*looking for approval to* PINTOR *and other*
    SAILORS, *who nod to him in confirmation of what*
    he says.)
                                    We've heard of that.
ESCOBAR.   You have ?—Why, then, you're all a set of
    fools.
PINTOR.   I've known that all along.   'Tis not our
    fault.
ESCOBAR.   Not ?—Whose?
PINTOR.   The government's.   It forced us here.
ESCOBAR.   But we're not kept here by it.   What
    does that
    Is one man's will, and he's a lunatic.
ROLDAN.   How did he ever gain the ear of Spain ?
ESCOBAR.   By talking.   Most men's thoughts are led,
    you know,
    In trains of their own talking.   Talk them down,
    They've lost their leader.   Keep on talking then,
    They'll find in you another.   Any sound
    You choose to make, they'll take for sense.   Why
    not ?
    It's grown to be a habit with them.
PINTOR.   Oh,
    'Tis not through talk or thought he deals with
        us,
    But force.
ESCOBAR.   Ay, and he'll find before he dies
    That men accept one's estimate of them.
    If he esteem them thinkers, give them thought,

They'll turn to him like thinking beings : but
If he esteem them brutes, and give them force,
They'll turn upon him like a brute.

ROLDAN. Who'll turn ?—
Ourselves ?

ESCOBAR. Why not ?—if he deserve it ?

ROLDAN. But
If we should mutiny, and then go home—

ESCOBAR. The question's not between this place
and home ;
No, but the bottom of the sea and land.
And other lands are fertile as are Spain's.

PINTOR. Oh, you've no wife and children !

ESCOBAR. Humph, that means
My life is not behind me, but before—
With precious little left of that. And yet
What's life ?—what's time worth, if we've no good
times ?—
And he who squeezes these all out our life,—-
Wrings our last drop of sweat to serve himself,—
He deputies the devil, boss of despots.

ROLDAN. You're right. He doesn't care for us ?

ESCOBAR. What he
Cares for, is notoriety, and that's
The bulge of contrast. Crush and hush your kind,
You're seen and heard of.

PINTOR. Gad, what right has he
To gem and offset Genoese mastership
By making slaves of Spaniards ?

ROLDAN.   Ay, that's what
  They ask at home!
ESCOBAR.   Just what they'll ask again,
  If we sail home without him.
PINTOR.   That they will.
  Why, where's the man of station in the land
  Who'll not be glad to hear we've failed?
ESCOBAR.   And all
  The rest will see that, when we've sailed beyond
  All others on a sea like this, we've done
  The whole that Spain could ask.
ROLDAN.   And still——
ESCOBAR.   As if
  'Twas not our duty, in a madman's hands,
  To use our reason, and resist him.
PINTOR.   Yes.
  One should assert his reason.   We're not brutes.
ESCOBAR.   We're worse than brutes in his view.
      Brutes, at times,
  To save their lives, will turn upon a man.
  But we—six score to one, but all afraid
  To call our souls our own.   Let him appear,
  We fly like cry-girls from a buzzing bug
  One touch could crush in no time.
ROLDAN.   But the court
  Has clothed him with authority.
ESCOBAR.   Mere sheep
  Would not be driven by another sheep
  Though clothed in bear-skin, could they only hear
  His old familiar bleat.

ROLDAN.   And yet you know
   He has the power——
ESCOBAR.   Because we give it him,
   Who whine,—whine merely like a set of babes,
   Too weak to lift a finger for ourselves.
ROLDAN. The King——
ESCOBAR.   Oh, he's divine! I grant it; ay,
   What else could ever pick out, plying but
   A random sword, and prick and pin in place
   As many Spanish cowards as are here?
ROLDAN. Man, you will have us hung for murder
      yet.
ESCOBAR. There's many a way that one can kill a
      cat.
   The best I know is drowning. Nights are dark,
   And one may slip against a man, and he,
   When slipped against, may tumble overboard.
   If so, he drowns—but how?—he drowns himself.
ROLDAN. He's coming—Hark! We—Down—Let's
      clear from this.
         *Exeunt—Right Center—*ROLDAN, PINTOR
            and ESCOBAR.
      *Enter—Left Side Second—*COLUMBUS.
COLUMBUS (*to himself*).
   He comes on plotting.—That is plain enough.
   How form and face—mere garments that they
      are—
   Will siss and wrinkle to a twist of thought!—
   Fools!—Yet without fools, where were sovereignty

For wise men ?   'Twould be harder work than 'tis
To do earth's thinking for it ; harder work
To string the nerves that center in one's brain
Through all the mass, and rein it to one's will.—
Can I do this with these men ? or must I,
I who have given all these years to it,
Ay, and my young love too, my life, my all,—
Must I turn back ?—I will not,though they kill me.
      (*Looking at paper in his hand.*)
This reckoning shows seven hundred fifty leagues.
'Twas well I made a false one for the crew.
Already that's six hundred.   Humph, without it
I might have had more trouble.   In the time
I served King Renier, and was sent to take
The galley Fernandina ; and my crew,
In fright to hear two ships were guarding her,
Had turned our helm, and thought we flew away;
Ah, how I steered straight for her in the night !
And fought her at the dawn !—I'll do so here.
We men who think, have duties due our kind.
One duty is, to block their finding out
What are our thoughts, for fear they'll know too
    much.
The truth is not a plaything for a babe.
The truth's a gem, and sometimes needs encasing.
Yet, if we sail on long, the day will come
When our true distance must be known.—What,
    then ?
What then ?

VOICES (*beyond Left Side Rear*). He shall turn back!
    He shall! We'll make him.

COLUMBUS. Hark! hark! turn back? They dare
    speak out like that?
  Oh, what a cruel destiny is mine
  To unfulfillment doom'd, if I do not
  What even heaven itself has never done,—
  Give patience to a world of restlessness!
  Oh, God, I think I serve thee. Give me power
  To calm these minds, as Christ made calm the
    sea.

*Enter —Left Side Rear—*ESCOBAR, ROLDAN, PIN-
  TOR, SANCHEZ, GUTIERREZ, *and others.*
  What's wrong, my men?

ESCOBAR.   We came to tell you, sir,
  'Tis time that we turn back.

COLUMBUS.   Turn back?
  A strange idea that!

SEVERAL.   Oh, strange! oho!

COLUMBUS.   Why yes,
  With what we've seen to-day—the herbs and
    flowers.

PINTOR. We've seen them many a day.

COLUMBUS.   But not the same—
  Not fresh and green; and then the small shore-
    fish
  And birds too, birds of kinds that never sleep,
  Nor light, except on land—the singing birds
  That perched upon our mast.

ESCOBAR.   If there were land—
  It's been called out three times—we've passed it
    now.
COLUMBUS.   We're in a bay, perhaps.
ESCOBA.   You wouldn't steer
  As Pinzon wanted.
COLUMBUS.   No; the birds all flew
  This other way.   I thought them flying home.
PINTOR.   Well, we're not birds.
ESCOBAR.   We're going home though.
ROLDAN.   Yes.
COLUMBUS.   A pleasant swim !   This ship is going
    on.
SEVERAL.   No, no.
COLUMBUS.   Why, men, you've said the same
    before.
  Have you forgot how many of you cried,
  Ay, cried, in fear of burning skies above
  The Teneriffe volcano?—and I said
  It would not harm you.   Did it ?   Then shot by
  That meteor ; and I said it too would pass.
  Did I mistake ?   Then tireless western winds ;
  But east winds turned them.   Then a glassy sea ;
  But billows broke it.   Then these signs of land ;
  And now they multiply, as I had hoped.
  If so far I've been right, I've earned your trust.
ESCOBAR.   Ugh !   Those are old tales now.
SEVERAL.   Yes.
COLUMBUS.   Let them be.

The land toward which we sail is not unknown;
And those who've seen it say, were all the gold
In all of Europe grouped and fused to make
A single mass, 'twould hardly form one cliff
Of endless mountain ranges that are there.

ROLDAN.   Hear that now!

COLUMBUS.   They would be enough to make
A lord, at home, of every one of you
Without the title ; but, think you, the court,
The courtiers, would not wish you this besides?
You, who had burned through unknown darkness
    here
More brilliantly than comets through the sky?——
I mean it, for the trail you leave behind
Will write in deathless light around the world
The endless glory of our Christian Spain.

ROLDAN and OTHERS.   Yes, yes.

ESCOBAR.   No, no, come on!

(*Moving toward* COLUMBUS, *and urging others to do
    the same*).

PINTOR (*to* ROLDAN *and those who hold back*).   You're
    pledged to us.
    Lay hands upon him.   Make him yield.

COLUMBUS (*as* ESCOBAR *gets near him*).
                                Stand back.
    I represent the king.

ESCOBAR.   We're not your slaves.

COLUMBUS. Far better so than slaves to one
    another.

Lay hands on me, 'twill not be I alone
Have six score masters.   Look you to your mates.
You've pledged yourselves to stand together?
    What?—
Have you, or you, no foe in all this crew?
And now you place your life in that foe's hands?
When all he needs to raise himself in Spain
Is to speak truth of you, —you think he'll not?
Ay, kill me, drown me, yet I'll be avenged.
When bad men band, 'tis traitors fill their camp;
And, if a fair foe fail, the foul will not,
For in that fight are God and devil both.

ROLDAN.   That's true.   I'll not be found here.
        (*Turning away with others*).

PINTOR.   No, nor I.

COLUMBUS (*aside*).   At last the tide has turned.
    Heaven help me now.
            (*to the sailors*).
I thought that I had officers and men
Too manly to see one man stand alone,—
That some would stand beside me.   Was I
    wrong?

SANCHEZ.   No.

GUTIERREZ.   No.

        (ROLDAN *and those with him come beside*
            SANCHEZ *and* GUTIERREZ. *They approach*
            COLUMBUS. ESCOBAR *falls back*).

COLUMBUS.   I thank you, men.   I hoped as much.
And now—why now you're my brave crew again.

You've been so brave, I could not bear to think
That you could fail of perfect victory
Here, too, almost in sight.   How you would feel
When, after that next voyage which now 'tis
    sure
That some one else would make, did we go
    home—
You saw the wreaths and wealth that you alone
Had really won, deck other heads and hands !

SANCHEZ. You're right.

ROLDAN.   Ay, ay.

COLUMBUS.   You had forgotten this.
Well, we'll forget what's happened here to-night.
You know, men, I'm in this same boat with you ;
And all that comes to you must come to me.

ROLDAN. That's true.

COLUMBUS.   Then let the matter rest.   Enough !
Now to your places.

       Exeunt Left Side Front—Left Side Rear—
       and Right Center—all except COLUMBUS,
       who watches them for a moment, then con-
       tinues speaking to himself

                One more crisis passed !
How many further ? — Lord, how long ! how long !
(*Kneels a moment, then rises and looks off over the sea.*)
Because an owl will gaze at darkness so,
It does not prove he sees—mere habit.   Ah !
    (*A slightly moving light appears through the*

*curtain backing at the Right, and another
steady light at the Left slightly different
from the first.* COLUMBUS *looks at the
first.)*

What's that?—a light?—'Tis not like Pinzon's?
No.
         (Looking at the light at the Left).
His Pinta's there—and yet—I thought—why yes.
              (Looking to the Left).
The Nina's here behind us.—Yet this light—
    (Looking again at the light at the Right).
It cannot be a star!—Am I deceived?
         (Beckoning to Left Side Rear.)
Here Pedro, Pedro Gutierrez.

         Enter—Left Side Rear GUTIERREZ.

GUTIERREZ.   Ay.
COLUMBUS (*pointing toward the Right Back*).
    Can you see anything off there?
GUTIERREZ.   Why yes—
    The Pinta.
COLUMBUS (*pointing to the Left Back*). No, the
    Pinta's here.
GUTIERREZ.   So 'tis.
    The Nina's gone ahead, then?
COLUMBUS (*pointing to Left*). No, look back.
GUTIERREZ. 'Tis some ship's light.
COLUMBUS.   You're sure 'tis not a star.
GUTIERREZ. How can it be?

COLUMBUS. There's Sanchez. I'll ask him.
Rodrego.
(*Calling to some one beyond Left Side Front*).
*Enter—Left Side Front—*SANCHEZ.
SANCHEZ. Eh, sir?
COLUMBUS (*pointing to the Right Back*).
Can you see that light?
SANCHEZ. Where?
COLUMBUS. There, beyond the Pinta's.
SANCHEZ. Yes. I thought
The Nina was behind us.
COLUMBUS (*pointing to the Left*).
So she is.
SANCHEZ. What? can another ship have sailed off
here?
COLUMBUS. Another ship, eh? Watch it further.
GUTIERREZ. Why,——
I think it moves.
SANCHEZ. It does!
COLUMBUS. Not up and down
As if on waves, but to and fro?
GUTIERREZ. Just so!
COLUMBUS. Yes, some long distance to and fro.
(*The light makes this motion.*)
SANCHEZ. Let's call
The others.
COLUMBUS. No, not yet, no false alarm!
GUTIERREZ. You think it land?
COLUMBUS (*nodding*). Inhabited by men.

GUTIERREZ.   By men ?—Good God !

COLUMBUS.   Yes, you may well say good.

GUTIERREZ.   I think I see what seems a line of surf.

COLUMBUS.   Perhaps.   If so, the Pinta's nearing it.
   It's almost daybreak.   We shall hear her gun.

SANCHEZ.   Your order that a false report would rob
   Its starter of a chance to take the prize
   Pledged to the first discoverer of the land,
   Will keep the signal back until they're sure.

COLUMBUS.   Best so !   If blind men all were born
     blind, none
   Were cursed by losing sight.   In nights like this,
   'Tis not unwakened hope I dread, so much
   As wakened disappointment.
          (The report of a gun is heard.)
                  What ? so soon ?

SANCHEZ.   You see 'tis true !

COLUMBUS.   No doubt of it !

GUTIERREZ.   No, none.
      *(The   stage   is   gradually   becoming   brighter
      with the approaching dawn.   Voices of the
      SAILORS are heard.)*

COLUMBUS.   The sailors !   I must go now.   You
   receive them ;
   And wait till I return.   An hour so grand
   As this is, should be welcomed fittingly.

Exit—Left Side Second—into the cabin, COLUMBUS.

*Enter—Right Center—from the hold—*ESCOBAR, ROL-
    DAN, PINTOR, *and others.*

Enter—Left Side Rear—others.

(ROLDAN *rushes to the Right, and gazes towards
where the light was first seen.*)

ESCOBAR.   A false report, of course !

PINTOR.   Of course, but then——

ROLDAN.   Good heavens, 'tis true !

ESCOBAR.   'Tis true ?

ROLDAN.   There's land.

ESCOBAR.   It can't be.

ROLDAN.   Yes it is.   Look there.

PINTOR (*contemptuously, after looking not exactly
    where* ROLDAN *points.*)   A cloud.

ROLDAN.   Cloud ?   No.   As clear as daylight, man.
    'Tis land.

ESCOBAR.   It is, hurrah !

PINTOR.   You think so ?

ESCOBAR.   Are you blind ?
    'Tis no mistake, it is land !

                (*to the other* SAILORS).

                                Boys, hurrah !

SAILORS.   Land, land !

ROLDAN.   No doubt of it !

SAILORS.   Hurrah !

*They embrace each other and make wild demonstra-
    tions of delight*).

ESCOBAR (*looking toward Left Side Second—and
    calling aloud*).

    The admiral !

ROLDAN.   Three cheers !

    8

PINTOR.   The admiral!

ROLDAN.   He does not know it yet?

SANCHEZ.   Trust him for that.

SAILORS (*shouting*).

The admiral! Hurrah! The admiral!

SANCHEZ. "All hail the Queen," now. That will
fetch him. Sing.

(*All remove their caps and chant the following*):

ALL HAIL THE QUEEN.[*]

All hail the Queen.
No thrills can fill the lover's breast
For that first love he loves the best,
Like ours that throb to each appeal
　　Of her in whom, enthroned above
The nation's heart, we see, we feel
　　The symbol of the sway we love,
　　The while we hail our Queen.

All hail the Queen,
No cause can rouse the soul of strife
In men who war for child and wife,
Like ours that, vowed to victory,
　　Know not of rest until above
The foe that falls, enthroned we see
　　The symbol of the sway we love,
　　The while we hail our Queen.

[*] "The crew were now assembled on the decks of the
several ships, to return thanks to God for their prosperous
voyage, and their happy discovery of land, chanting the Salve
Regina and other anthems. Such was the solemn manner in
which Columbus celebrated all his discoveries." (Irving's
Columbus: Book VI., Chap. I.)

All hail the Queen.
No loyalty can make a son
Show what a mother's love has done,
Like ours who press through land and sea,
Our one reward to find above.
Our gains that show what man can be,
The symbol of the sway we love,
The while we hail our Queen.

(*While this song is being sung, the scenery at the back of the stage moves from Right to Left, thus representing the gradual approach of the ship to land. Before the music ceases,* COLUMBUS *appears in full uniform on the Left above the cabin. He is clothed in scarlet. Behind him stands a standard-bearer holding aloft the royal standard, and on either side of this, two others hold the banners of the enterprise, emblazoned with a green cross flanked by the letters F and Y, the initials of Fernando and Isabel.* (*Irving's Columbus. Book* IV., *Chap.* I., *also Book* VI., *Chap.* I.)

ROLDAN (*catching sight of* COLUMBUS).
   See there !

ESCOBAR.   Ah, there he is.

SAILORS.   Hurrah ! hurrah !

ESCOBAR (*shouting to* COLUMBUS). Ay, you were right.
               'Tis here.

ROLDAN.   He's always right.

ESCOBAR.   I told you so.

ROLDAN (*aside to* ESCOBAR).

                    You did?—What time was that?

PINTOR.   The Admiral forever!

ROLDAN (*aside to* PINTOR).

                    Ay, since when?
                (Shouting aloud).

Now he'll remember who have been his friends.

ESCOBAR.   Ay, that he will.

ROLDAN.   We knew you would succeed.

PINTOR.   The greatest day that Spain has ever
    seen.

ESCOBAR.   Gained through the greatest men that
    Spain has had.

                (To the SAILORS.)

Here, swear him your allegiance.   Down, men,
    down.

        (All fall on their knees before COLUMBUS.)

COLUMBUS.   I thank you, men, both for myself and
    those

Who sent us forth; and join with you to swear

Allegiance to our sovereigns—more than this,

        (Pointing to cross upon the banner),

To that far higher Power that they too serve

Whose symbol is inscribed upon our banner.

In that we conquer.   When we disembark

'Twill be to plant the cross just where we land.

And now—you seem exultant—I confess

To awe like that which Moses must have felt

When God's own hand had touched him as it
    passed.

I cannot stand – nay, let me kneel with you

With praise, thanksgiving, and new-vowed devo-
    tion

    *(They all kneel beneath the standard, and
    while the scenery, moving behind, represents
    the approach to land, after a few mo-
    ments of silence, except for the music of the
    orchestra, they chant the following :)*

THE OLD TIMES GO, THE NEW SUCCEED.

The old times go, the new succeed,
    With changes none can stay.
The foremost fall, and all who lead ;
    Yet life moves on for aye.
But nevermore, whate'er be seen,
Will aught be what it would have been,
Had we not lived and done the deed
    That we have done to-day.

The forms we prize, the thoughts we heed,
    The laws our race obey ;
And all that loom in mount and mead
    And main will pass away.
But nevermore, whate'er be seen,
Will aught be what it would have been,
Had we not lived and done the deed
    That we have done to-day.

The years will leave all times of need,
　The soul will have her say,
The truth be throned, and love be freed,
　And heaven alone have sway.
But nevermore, whate'er be seen,
Will aught be what it would have been,
Had we not lived and done the deed
　That we have done to-day.

CURTAIN.

END OF ACT III.

ACT FOURTH.

SCENE FIRST.—*Reception room in a house at Palos.*
Entrances—Right Side and Left side.
*Enter—Left Side—*BEATRIX.
*Enter—Left Side—*COLUMBUS *and* DIEGO.

BEATRIX.   Returned?   Thank God!
COLUMBUS.   Yes, God alone could do it.
   (*to* DIEGO, *as voices are heard from without.*)
  For Pity's sake, Diego, send them off;
  And say that I to-night will tell them all.
         *Exit—Right Side—*DIEGO.
           (*to* BEATRIX.)
  And how's our son, Fernando?
BEATRIX.   Grown and strong.
  He's out just now   will not be back till noon.
  I thought you coming when I heard the noise.
COLUMBUS.   Ah, yes, as I remember, when I left,
  I roused a noise too.
BEATRIX.   You have roused one now
  That all the world will hear.
COLUMBUS.   You never praise
  A wind, because it makes the sea-waves roar;
  It may be empty, and it may do harm.
  I've learned to judge men's noises at their worth.

BEATRIX.   To think I ever joined with them against
    you !
COLUMBUS.   Why, what were woman's nature, void
    of fine
  Attemperment, adjusting it to form
  Society's barometer ?   You know
  Society is like the atmosphere :
  It's always round us, and it's all alike—
  All warm in sunshine and all chill in storm.
  You met me in my sunshine, saw me first
  Surrounded only by my friends.
BEATRIX.   If you
  Had heard the talk !
COLUMBUS.   I heard too much of it.
BEATRIX.   You found the land though !
COLUMBUS.   Yes, and such a land !
BEATRIX.   As fair as this ?
COLUMBUS.   A land of endless May,
  And set in seas transparent as their skies ;
  Where every kind of spice, grain, fruit and flower
  Teems in green valleys that need not be tilled,
  All crowned on high by mounts, whose gold and
    gems
  Lie on the surface.
BEATRIX.   And belong to you !—
  What joy to feel that now it all is over !
COLUMBUS.   All never will be over in this world.
  The great care passed trails little cares behind
  That aggregate no less of worry.

BEATRIX.   True ;
But when the land was found——
COLUMBUS.   One ship was wrecked ;
And twice returning, too, we all seemed lost.
If so, the whole would have been lost that now
We've found.
BEATRIX.   And then ?
COLUMBUS.   I vowed a pilgrimage,
Wrote out our story.   Like the wine it was,
I sealed it in a cask, and let it float.
BEATRIX.   But reached the land !
COLUMBUS.   Yes, first at the Azores
As wet as fish, too.   That was why, perhaps,
The Portuguese there spread their nets for us,
And not their tables.
BEATRIX.   Nets?
COLUMBUS.   To trap us, yes.
BEATRIX.   But why?
COLUMBUS.   To get our charts, resail our course,
And claim the credit of it.
BEATRIX.   They could not
Have been successful.
COLUMBUS.   Not if we had lived.
BEATRIX.   But yet —
COLUMBUS.   No but !   Our ship was driven next
To Portugal itself—by accident.
Of course : a storm came on—and there the court
Were soft as cats are, when they play with mice.

The fur, though, did not wholly glove the claw,
Nor cloak a plot to murder us.   It failed.
Instead, Francisco de Almeida sails,
With secret orders from the envious court,
To cross the sea, and make our gain his own.

BEATRIX.   But Spain will right you, give you titles?
   —fame? —

COLUMBUS.   Oh, 'tis not that!

BEATRIX.   But wealth will come with them.

COLUMBUS.   If I had worked for these, I had not
   lived
The life I have.

BEATRIX.   If you've not worked for them in part, at
   least,
You're not the man I thought.

COLUMBUS.   How so?

BEATRIX.   You mean that you could tamely waive
   Your rights—your children's too—to fame and
   wealth?

COLUMBUS.   I see—I had not thought.

BEATRIX.   Oh, yes; your mind
   Is so ideal, so filled with its own thoughts,
   They crowd out thoughts for others.

COLUMBUS.   Think you so?
I must correct the fault.

BEATRIX.   You'll now have time.
How sweet to settle down upon your honors!

COLUMBUS.   What, what?—You think that I'm prepared for that?

BEATRIX. Why, you're not young.

COLUMBUS. I'm fifty-eight.

BEATRIX. Not strong.

COLUMBUS. To-day there came a letter from the
    sovereigns.
  It begs my presence to prepare with them
  A second expedition.

BEATRIX. What! another?—
  You'll go?

COLUMBUS. Why not?

BEATRIX. You've earned the right to rest.

COLUMBUS. From whence?—I do not feel it given
    me here.

        (Placing his hand on his heart.)

BEATRIX. You're not content yet?—What an ap-
    petite
  Has man's ambition! All that gluts to-day
  But bringing greater hunger for the morrow;
  A fire consuming all it feeds upon,
  Still flaming upward and beyond it all.

COLUMBUS. That's true of more than you apply it
    to, —
  Of those desires that are but of the soul.
  I sailed to find the Indies. They're not found;
  To plant the cross in all those lands; and yet
  Great lands wait undiscovered.

BEATRIX. Other ships
  Are sure to sail and reach them.

COLUMBUS. Ay, they may.

But all that I can know is that the call
Has come to me.
BEATRIX.   Well, well, if you say must,
Perhaps it must be.   Still—if you are needed—
You know you are—there's one thing : you can make
Your own terms with the sovereigns.

*Enter—Right—*DIEGO.

COLUMBUS.   What ?
BEATRIX.   Your terms—
Demand your rights, and mine—your son's and mine.

Enter—Left—a MAID *who speaks aside to* BEATRIX.

DIEGO *(aside)*. There's nothing like a she-hand, skill'd in needles,
To frock and fringe a man's unmanliness
In rags of failure.   When unselfish zest
Demands investment in the mail of force,
Farewell good-fellowship that cheers the ranks :
The private favorite's prince of public envy.
    (*To* BEATRIX *who is looking toward him.*)
Oh, he'll be wealthy as a king ere long.
That ought to satisfy you.
(*To* COLUMBUS, *referring to the crowd outside the house.*)   Yes, I sent
Them off.
BEATRIX (*to the two men, as she turns from talking to the* MAID).
        I'm wanted, please excuse me.

BEATRIX *bows to* COLUMBUS *and* DIEGO, *and*
          they bow to her. As BEATRIX *turns away,*
          DIEGO *begins to talk aside to* COLUMBUS,
          shaking his head as if disapproving of
          what she has just said. BEATRIX *pauses*
          near Right Side Entrance—to say aside—
                                        Now,

I'll write at once to Dona Bobadilla,
And have her tell the Queen our terms—Ours ?—
     yes—
Why, I've been told a thousand times or more
That what I wish, he wishes. They are ours.

*Exeunt—Right—*BEATRIX *and* MAID, *who has waited*
          for her just before the door.

DIEGO (*to* COLUMBUS *as if continuing a conversation*).
     We'll waive that then.—Now tell me of the people.
COLUMBUS.   A noble race, who live there in a state
     Almost of Paradise, their wants so few
     And nature so profuse--I tell you truth—
     They neither toil nor spin.
DIEGO.   Nor spin ? Why how
     About their clothing ?
COLUMBUS.   They don't need it.
DIEGO.   What ?
COLUMBUS.   Oh, you get used to that !
DIEGO.   You do ? —then what's
     Their character ?
COLUMBUS.   That's not so much a thing
     Of clothes as civilization thinks, perhaps.

DIEGO.   But then——

COLUMBUS.   The Turks keep faces veiled; turn all
The body into private parts—what's gained ?
If ill-desire be fruit of thought that's germed
In curiosity, to clear away
Some underbrush, and let in light might help
To blight the marsh-weed, and reveal, besides,
Part of the beauty that brought bliss to Eden.

DIEGO.   You mean——

COLUMBUS.   There's nothing like a length of robe,
Material in substance and in sense,
To stole an anti-spirit-ministry.
It bags what heaven made that the world may
    deem
The bag well baited for a game of hell.

DIEGO.   You talk in riddles.

COLUMBUS.   Read a page or two
From human nature, they'll be solved. Out
    there,
Except with chiefs—it is the same, you know,
With our high classes—people live in pairs,
As birds do ; and, myself, I saw no hint
Of lust or competition. They all seem
To love their neighbors as themselves, and own
All things in common. Why, to us they gave
Whatever we could ask ; and often too
Without the dimmest prospect of return.

DIEGO.   They welcomed you ?

COLUMBUS.   They thought us fresh from heaven.

You know they're copper-colored. We looked
    white.

Oh, what a race to be made Christians of!

DIEGO. What for?

COLUMBUS. Why, only give such men religion ——

DIEGO. With lives of love, and welcoming guests
    from heaven—

Where would you find much more in Christian
    Spain?

COLUMBUS. Well, but——

DIEGO.   Precisely what I mean—a butt.

COLUMBUS. You're always butting some thing,
    brother.

DIEGO.   Yes,

A family trait with both of us, I think.

Were I a man of action like yourself,

I might not doubt but do.

COLUMBUS.   Not undo, eh?—

You mean you doubt my statements?

DIEGO.   Hardly that,

But I was thinking——

COLUMBUS.   That's a dangerous thing.

DIEGO. Yes, but for it I should have been a priest.

At present, I'm confessor but to you.

And my advice is, never to repeat

What you've just said.

COLUMBUS.   Why not?

DIEGO.   'Tis sure to make

The world suspect you.

COLUMBUS.   How?—and what?

DIEGO.   Why, say,
Your faith.

COLUMBUS. Impossible! God knows—they know—
The purpose of my life.

DIEGO.   Your life! But faith—
That's not a thing to-day of life, but talk;
And God—He has not much to do with it.
A man of faith, is one whose faith in those
To whom he's talking, makes him talk their
    thoughts.
None here will think that what you say can be.

COLUMBUS. Not even you?

DIEGO.   Why, yes.—but yes and no.
The power that makes imagination burst
Through limits of our world, as you have done,
To find this new world, makes it pass beyond
    them.
The glories of that sunset land may all
Be in the land you saw, or in the sky.

COLUMBUS. I see your meaning.
            *Enter—*BEATRIX—*Right.*

DIEGO.   '   If your mounts of gold too
Do not come tumbling very speedily
To fill the itching lap of Spain, why then,
There's some one will be blamed.

COLUMBUS.   Oh, but they will!

BEATRIX. Now, gentlemen, if you will walk in here
            (*Motioning toward the Right*),

We'll have some luncheon; and I've news for
    you,
Both bright and black.

COLUMBUS.   There's nothing bright can come,
But brings behind it something in the shade.

BEATRIX. The court, so Dona Bobadilla writes,
Will welcome you in state at Barcelona.

DIEGO. They're bright in doing that! Now what's
    the black?

BEATRIX. That Pinzon's ship has reached Bayonne;
    and there
The man has claimed your honors as his own.

COLUMBUS. What perfidy!—determined to turn
    back
Before we found the land, and after that
Deserting us.

DIEGO.   To herald his delight
In what he made you do!—I'm not surprised.
The train of genius marshals everywhere
Distrust before success, and envy after.

Exeunt—at the Right—BEATRIX, COLUMBUS *and*
    DIEGO.

SCENE SECOND.—*A grand temporary Pavilion, erected
in front of the royal residence at Barcelona. In the
extreme background, beyond an open place, is the exterior of the house of Cardinal Mendoza. In front*
  9

*of this house, are awnings or curtains, which, at the
conclusion of* SCENE SECOND, *are to be lifted or drawn
aside in order to prepare for* SCENE THIRD. *To the
Right are parts of the Palace, to the Left are pillars
supporting the Pavilion. Within the Pavilion, at the
Left, near the back of stage but in front of the open
place, is an elevated platform on which are four throne
chairs. Nearer the Left Front of the stage is a place
for a choir.*

*Entrances :—Right Side Rear—into the open place be-
yond the Palace—Right Side Front—in front of the
Palace; Left Side Rear—open place beyond the Pavilion—Left Side Middle—between the pillars at the
Left—and Left Side Front—in front of the Pavilion.*

The curtain rising discloses the KING *and* QUEEN
and PRINCE JUAN, *seated upon the throne, attended
by the dignitaries of their court and the principal
nobility of* Castile, Valentia, Catalonia *and* Aragon :
also GONZALEZ, ARANA, FONSECA, BREVIESCA *and
others. The royal choir are at the extreme Left Front,
and spectators of the more common sort at the Right
and in the Rear. All seem enthusiastic.*

Music by orchestra and choir, with the following words :

HAIL TO THE HERO, HOME FROM STRIFE.

Hail to the hero, home from strife,
Pride of our hearts and hope of our life,
Hail to his glancing crest and plume,
Flashed like lightning into the gloom.

Hail to the grit that, lost to view,
Out of the darkness brought him through,
Sprout of the slough-pit, bud of the thorn,
    After the night
    The light of the morn.
Crown him with flowers and have them bright.
Crown him, the man of the land's delight.

Hail to the hero, home from strife,
Pride of our hearts and hope of our life.
Hail to the ring of the voice that taught
Drumming and roaring the rhythm of thought.
Hail to the tones that turned to a cheer
Groan and shriek of a startled fear.
Hushing to rills the flood that whirred,
    Chorusing night
    With songs of the bird.
Shout him a welcome, and shout with might.
Shout for the man of the land's delight.

*Enter—Right side Rear—during the song, the follow-
ing procession :*

First come SOLDIERS *who march across the stage
to Left Side Rear—then halt, turn toward
the audience, and stand on guard at the
Rear. Next comes an officer who turns
toward the Pavilion, marching in front of
it, and down the Right.—Following him are
Indians brought from America. They are
painted according to their savage fashion,
and decorated with their national orna-*

*ments of gold. As they and those follow-
ing them approach the pavilion, each in turn
salutes the* KING *and* QUEEN *who remain
sitting. After the Indians, come men bearing various kinds of parrots together with
stuffed birds and animals of unknown
species and rare plants supposed to be of
precious qualities. A display is also made
of Indian coronets, bracelets, and other
decorations of gold. After this, surrounded
by a brilliant throng of Spanish cavaliers,
comes* COLUMBUS. *He is on horseback,
but dismounts at the entrance of the pavilion and enters it. As he does so, the* KING
and QUEEN *both rise to welcome him.*
COLUMBUS *kneels, the* KING *instantly takes
his hand and motions to him to seat himself in the vacant chair beside them on the
slightly elevated platform. He is the only
one besides the* KING, QUEEN *and* PRINCE
who is seated.

(See Irving's COLUMBUS: *Book V.
Chapter VI.)*

*Enter—Right Side Front—*DIEGO *and* BEATRIX, *and
stand watching the ceremonies.*

KING *(just as* COLUMBUS *seats himself beside him).*
Well done, thou good and faithful servant.

QUEEN. Yes.
The land was where you said.

COLUMBUS. 'Twas within less
Than eighty leagues of where I reckoned it.

QUEEN. A rich land too?

COLUMBUS (*motioning to the attendants who bring forward an exhibit, as he mentions them, the different objects which they are carrying*).

You see what we have brought : —
These birds and animals unknown to Spain,
All promising vast wealth in plumes and furs :
These trees and plants that grow like reeds in
swamps,
And covered thick as leaves with ready food :
These aromatic herbs, in which all forms
Of sickness find a sure and natural cure :
This gold that lies upon the soil like dust,
Or else like pebbles tumbling from the cliffs,
And easily moulded into ornaments :
These pearls and gems that line the river-beds ;
Add these brave people, sons of God like us,
With generous natures and compliant wills,
Who met us kneeling, as we knelt on shore,
With reverent souls prepared by heaven itself
To welcome us as heavenly messengers :
And who to be made whole in holiness
Need but the cleansing water of the church.
Are these not eloquent beyond the power
Of mortal lips ?

QUEEN.　　　　They are.

KING.　　　　　　They are.

ALL.　　　　　　　　Yes, yes.

COLUMBUS. But what that land contains is in
　　supply
　As far beyond the treasure here, as is
　A whole vast continent beyond the store
　That can be packed in one small vessel.　Yes,
　That realm of boundless wealth in rock and soil
　And boundless progress for the state and soul,
　Past all that human fancy can conceive,
　Lies there, embed in crystal seas and skies,
　A wondrous gift, fresh from the hand of God,
　As if untarnished by the touch of man,
　Awaiting your most Christian Majesties.

KING. Give God the praise.

QUEEN.　　　　　　Thank God.

PEOPLE.　　　　　　　Amen, amen.

KING. Columbus, all the people speaks their
　　thanks.
　We but fulfill their wishes, crowning you
　With every proof of royal approbation.
　We now decree that, through all time henceforth,
　You shall be known as Admiral, Viceroy,
　And, if once more you'll cross the sea for us,
　Commander-General of all armaments,
　And Governor of all realms awaiting there,
　The bearer of the royal seal, with power
　To name your own successor and to will

Your own inheritance; and evermore
These arms here are decreed your family.

Enter—Left Side Second—an attendant bearing
a banner in which the royal arms, the
castle and lion, are quartered with a group
of islands surrounded by waves and under
them the motto :

" *To Castile and Leon*
Columbus gave a new world."

(*See Irving's* COLUMBUS : *Book* V. *Chapter* VII.)

DIEGO (*at the extreme Right Front—to* BEATRIX).
You think he needed all those titles?

BEATRIX.   Why?

DIEGO.   I think they sound like you.

BEATRIX.   Well, what of that?

DIEGO.   When I've been hunting, I have found that
        birds
    Of brightest plumage are the soonest shot.
    This is a world where many men go shooting.

KING (*continuing to* COLUMBUS).
    And more than this : of all the ships in Spain
    We authorize your choice of which you will,
    With power to force each captain, pilot, crew,
    Or owner of a vessel, arms or stores,
    To do your bidding ; and besides we pledge
    Two-thirds of all the royal revenues
    Derived from our church tithes, and all that comes
    From confiscating all the property
    Of all the Jews, whom now, to yield us this,
    We banish from our realm.

PEOPLE (*with fervor and exultation*).
                            God bless the king!
FONSECA.   God bless your Christian Majesties!
OTHERS.   God bless!
COLUMBUS.   You do me honor, overmuch, I fear.
  And I too would give praise where all is due :
  And that with deeds, not words.   In view, this day,
  Of all the wealth that, with the power you give,
  Is certain now to come to me, I vow
  To raise and arm, inside of twice four years,
  Four thousand horse and twice as many foot,
  And just as many more in five years more,
  To drive to death the heathen Saracen
  And wrest from him the Holy Sepulchre.
PEOPLE.   Oh, God! we thank thee!
OTHERS.   Glory to the Lord!
KING.   Now let us, all together, seek the church,
  And praise Him, as is meet for these vast boons
  Vouchsafed to Christian Spain, there to convert
                (*Motioning toward the* INDIANS.)
  By holy baptism these heathen souls.
ARANA (*to* FONSECA, *exultingly*).
  The day begins when all the earth and all
  Its wealth shall be converted unto us.
*Exeunt—Left Side Front—*KING, QUEEN, PRINCE,
        COLUMBUS. *Courtiers, Indians, etc.*
*Exeunt—Right Side Front—*DIEGO, BEATRIX *and
                others.*
(*While the rest are leaving the choir chant as follows :*)

Oh soul, what earthly crown
Is bright as his renown
Whose tireless race
Outruns the world's too halting pace,
To reach beyond the things men heed
A truth that all behind him need!

Oh soul, what man can be
As near to Christ as he
Who looks to life
Not first for fame and last for strife ;
But shuns no loss nor pain whereby
To lift the truth and lower the lie !

Exeunt—Left Side Front—Choir.
Awnings in front of the house of MENDOZA *rise reveal
ing Scene Third*

SCENE THIRD : *Interior of a banqueting hall in the
house of* MENDOZA. *A table crosses the stage at the
Rear. Behind it in the Center, on a seat slightly
raised above the rest, is* COLUMBUS. *At the right
end of the table is* MENDOZA : *at the left end,*
FONSECA *and* BREVIESCA. *Others arranged as
suits convenience.*

BREVIESCA (*to* FONSECA).

What native here has ever yet received
Such royal honors ?—Why, the sovereigns both
Stood up to greet him, hesitated, too,
To let him kneel, and sat him in their presence.

FONSECA. Here too he's on a throne.

BREVIESCA.   I never saw
  A Spaniard treated thus.
FONSECA.   He takes it all
  As if his due.
BREVIESCA.   Hold on.   I'll put him down—
  In thought, at least.
(*To* COLUMBUS, *who sits playing with an egg on the
                   table.*)
                    Say, Admiral, do you think
  If you had not made this discovery
  That there's no man in Spain who could have
      done it ?
COLUMBUS.   Why, that's a new idea.
MENDOZA.   So it is.
COLUMBUS.   I never asked myself about that yet—
  Oh, by the way, can any of you here
  Make this thing stand on end ?
        (GONZALEZ, BREVIESCA *and* FONSECA *begin to
            experiment, as do others, with eggs lying
            on the table near them.*)
FONSECA.   An egg ?
COLUMBUS.   An egg.
MENDOZA.   Can it be done ?
COLUMBUS.   Why, yes, you try it.
MENDOZA (*trying*).   No;
  I give it up.
FONSECA.   And I.
COLUMBUS (*to* BREVIESCA).
                    You give it up ?

BREVIESCA Why—yes—I don't see——

COLUMBUS (*setting the egg down on its small end with
enough force to break the shell and make it
stand*).

Now you see it—there!

MENDOZA. Oho!

BREVIESCA. That's nothing!

COLUMBUS. Yes, like other things,
"Tis easy enough, when once you've seen it done.
(*Laughter.*)

CURTAIN.

ACT FIFTH.

Scene First:—*A camp on the Island of Hispaniola. Backing, a clearing, amid woods with thick forests in the distance. At Right and Left, trees: at the Left near the Front, the hut of* Columbus. *Entrances Right Side Rear, Second and Front—between trees: Left Side Rear—behind the hut of* Columbus; *Left Side Second—from inside of it, Left Side Front—between trees.*

Enter—Right Side Rear— Escobar *and* Gamez.

Escobar. Ojeda, when his boats were on the coast,
Said that at home the Admiral's cause was lost.
Our notes have reached there. They've found
    out, at last,
How Spaniards, ay, and Spanish nobles too,
Are lorded over by this Genoese.

Gamez. And now you say he's superseded?

Escobar.   Yes,
By Bobadilla.

Gamez.   Who is he?

Escobar.   Enough,
If he's a Spaniard.

Gamez.   Strange, though, all the same!

Escobar. 'Tis said Breviesca and his bishop there,
Fonseca, they rule everything to-day.

'Twas they, you know, who got the crown to give,
Ojeda all the Admiral's charts and half
His rights too ; and would grant indulgences
Without a stint if they could have their way
To any here who struck him down.

GAMEZ.   Why so?

ESCOBAR.   You've never heard about his impudence,
When brought before the bishops, years ago ?

GAMEZ.   At Salamanca, yes : but he was right.

ESCOBAR.   Or how he knocked down Breviesca,
when
Fonseca's messenger ?—Besides, who wants
To blacken Spain with shade from Genoa?
Well, Bobadilla's landed now ; and when
His troopers flash in sight here, why, these eyes
That have been aching so to see him come
Will scratch some blinks to cure their vision's
itching.

Enter—Right Side—an old INDIAN, *and advances
toward* ESCOBAR, *who addresses him.*

Humph ! Who are you, old cove ?—What ?—
Clear the air.
Stand off a white man's shadow.

INDIAN.   Me would see
The Admiral.

ESCOBAR.   Use your eyes then.   Are you blind ?

INDIAN.   Me thought you know——

*Enter—Left Side Rear—*COLUMBUS, *and stands behind the three.*

Escobar.   Well, you've no right to think.
  And if we know, 'tis not our business
  To do your errands for you.
(Indian, *seeing* Columbus, *passes toward Left Side
          Rear.*)
Gamez   (*laughingly to* Escobar).
                              Settled him.
Columbus (*to* Indian).
                  What's this?
Indian (*to* Columbus).
                  Me wants to see you.
Columbus   (*motioning toward his cabin*).
                              Yes, but wait
  In there a moment, please.
Exit — Left Side — into the hut of Columbus, *the*
    Indian. Columbus *goes on to* Escobar.
                              It would be wise
  To keep the red-men friends : and friendship's light
  Reflects but what is kindled in ourselves.
  Extinguish it within, and soon without
  We find our world in darkness.—Now, to work.
  The trenches must be dug, and no delay.
  There's danger of attack.
Gamez.   I'm not a man
  For work like that.
Columbus.   Like what?
Escobar.   The work that lets
  These common laborers wipe their dirty paws
  Upon one's coat.

COLUMBUS. Then take it off.

GAMEZ. Ay, ay;
And grovel at their level.

COLUMBUS. Does your rank
Depend upon your coat?—pray heaven that you
Be born again, a new man and a true one.

GAMEZ. You did not promise this work, when we
sailed.

COLUMBUS. The Spaniards had not shown their
lust and greed,
Defiled the native women, killed the men,
And, sent in squadrons to preserve the peace,
All grasping for the whole of all they saw,
Beset their comrades like a set of bulls
Becrimsoned with each other's gore. Mere
brutes!
No wonder they have disenchanted thus
The people who at first believed them gods.
Now get you gone—no waiting!
(COLUMBUS *turns toward his hut.*)

ESCOBAR (*aside, shaking his fist at* COLUMBUS's *back*).
Yes, until
We get you gone, which'll not be very long.
*Exeunt—Right Side—*GAMEZ *and* ESCOBAR.

COLUMBUS (*going to his cabin and motioning the*
INDIAN *to come out.*)
Well now, my friend, what is it?

INDIAN. White man kill
Our men and steal our women.

COLUMBUS.   Yes—and I?

INDIAN.   Kill white man.

COLUMBUS.   What?

*Enter—Left Side Rear—*BARTHOLOMEW, *and stands
                by* COLUMBUS.

INDIAN.   We Injun call you men
     Great-Spirit-men.   Poor Injun when he die.
     When bad go here, when good go there,
               (*Pointing first down and then up.*)

COLUMBUS.   What, you—
     You Indians think this?

BARTHOLOMEW.   I shall write that home.
     'Tis more than some there seem to think.

COLUMBUS.   It is.
                    (*To* INDIAN.)
     And what of that, my friend?

INDIAN.   White-spirit-chief
     Send bad men here and good men there.
               (*Pointing first down and then up*).

COLUMBUS.   I see—
     Put down the bad, put up the good.   Yes, yes;
     You're right.   I'll try to learn the lesson, friend.

INDIAN (*pointing in a half-frightened way toward the
          Right*).
     Bad man come there.
               (BARTHOLOMEW *steps toward the Right*).

COLUMBUS.   Humph, humph, please leave us then;
     And wait in here again.
               (*Motioning toward his hut.*)

Exit—Left Side—into the hut, INDIAN. COLUMBUS
turns toward BARTHOLOMEW.

        Whom have we coming?

BARTHOLOMEW.   A crowd of captives—women, as I
    think.

  The men with them are Roldan's.

COLUMBUS.   'Twill be hard

  To deal with them. They're all old criminals.

  Suppose you bring a guard here.

BARTHOLOMEW.   Yes, I will.

       *Exit—Left Side Front—*BARTHOLOMEW.

COLUMBUS (*looking toward the Right.*)

  There's one of them seems coming on alone.

  That's fortunate.—Aha, and Pintor, too!

*Enter—Right Side—*PINTOR.   COLUMBUS *speaks to*
him.

  You back? What have you brought?

PINTOR.   Some household gods.

COLUMBUS.   Whose are they?

PINTOR.   Ours.

COLUMBUS.   Oh, yours?—how came they yours?

PINTOR.   By right of conquest.

COLUMBUS.   What?

PINTOR.   We killed their men.

COLUMBUS.   And left them widows?

PINTOR.   No; we made them brides.

  That's better than to leave them wives; not so?

COLUMBUS.   Law-breakers!

   10

PINTOR.   Pugh ! with all that you have seized,
Made slaves of, sent to Spain and sold ——
COLUMBUS.   But they were captives from our foes.

> *Enter — Left Side Rear — BARTHOLOMEW,*
> *GUTIERREZ and a guard who cross the*
> *stage at the back, and march forward*
> *between PINTOR and the Right Side.*

PINTOR.   Well I
Take any man who flushes red all over,
As they do when I'm coming, as a foe.
COLUMBUS.   The slaves we sent to Spain were taken
          there
To be made Christians of.
PINTOR.   And so with us—
We're Christians, aren't we ?—Well, we'll have
          them washed
And not made slaves, but take them to our
          homes,
And let them lead a free and easy life.
COLUMBUS.   And don't you see the danger? Why,
          their tribe
Will massacre us all : if not, your vices
Will bring you hell here, even while you live.
PINTOR.   You know my story—was condemned to
          death—
For nothing, though—and then the court decreed,
Instead of this, that I should come out here :
And if I make it hell, it seems to me,
That's where they want me.

COLUMBUS (*to* GUTIERREZ).

Take this man,
Search him for arms, and march him to the works.
(*To* PINTOR.)
Hereafter keep a hold upon your tongue.

PINTOR. Ay, ay, sir; but you'll not be hard on me.
This land needs peopling.

*Exit—Right Side—*GUTIERREZ *and* SOLDIERS
with PINTOR.

BARTHOLOMEW. It will need it more,
If Spain sends more of those vile wretches here.
We'll all be murdered then.

COLUMBUS. We may, as 'tis.

BARTHOLOMEW. Had I my way, a brute forever
kicking
Against the law should go in bit and bridle;
Ay, ay, to see a surgeon too. A touch
Of horse-play—that's a cutting that would cure
him
And all his kind. The best should let their land
Be peopled only by the best.

COLUMBUS. That might
Be wise; but where, pray, would you find the
best?
'Tis hard to tell which curse a country most:—
Its gentlemen who feel above all work;
Or workers so far down they feel beneath
All obligation to be gentlemen.
As for the first, heaven grant they'll soon find out

That this new world is not a place for them.
As for the second, if we plan no way
To keep them on the other side the sea,
Farewell to all the good we hope for here.

    *Enter—Right Side—*GUTIERREZ.

What now ?

GUTIERREZ (*handing* COLUMBUS *a note*).

    We found this when we searched him.

COLUMBUS.   Ay ?
 But it's not mine.

GUTIERREZ. Perhaps it might be well
 For you to read it.

COLUMBUS (*reading it*).

    So ?—I will.—What's this ?

   (*To* BARTHOLOMEW.)

 Bartholomew, a new conspiracy !

BARTHOLOMEW. But that man couldn't write.

COLUMBUS.   Oh no; but then,
 You see he carries it from one who can.

   (*Handing the note to* BARTHOLOMEW.)

 This time, it seems the high and low will meet,
 And we, between them, will be crushed.

BARTHOLOMEW (*threateningly*).   Perhaps.

COLUMBUS. It speaks about another fleet in port.
 I thought the treachery that had given my charts
 And right to govern islands west of here
 To Pinzon and Ojeda was enough.
 This speaks of one who claims a jurisdiction
 In our own island.

BARTHOLOMEW. Bobadilla, yes.
  What will you do?
COLUMBUS. Divide and conquer.
      (*To* GUTIERREZ.) Here!
GUTIERREZ. Ay, ay.
COLUMBUS. To chains with all those named in this.
        (*Handing* GUTIERREZ *the note.*)
  They're mostly in their homes now. Be alert.
        *Exit—Right Side—*GUTIERREZ.
          (*To* BARTHOLOMEW).
  Bartholomew, the rest of those condemned
  For sharing in that last conspiracy,
  Whom our too willing clemency has spared,
  Must be brought out to-day and hung.
BARTHOLOMEW. But then——
COLUMBUS. I see no other way. When mercy fails
  The cause is lost that does not call on justice.
            (*Noises outside.*)
  What noise is that—a tumult?
BARTHOLOMEW (*who with* COLUMBUS *looks toward*
    Left Side). No; they're cheers.
COLUMBUS. You make them out?
BARTHOLOMEW. Why, all the town is there!
  And look—our prisoners too!
COLUMBUS. What—those condemned
  To death?
BARTHOLOMEW. Ay, ay: and have the leadership;
  And with them—can it be?—'tis true! there come
  The St. Domingo traitors.

COLUMBUS. Is that so?
(*Looking toward Right Side.*)
Here, here!
*Enter—Right Side—*GUTIERREZ *with the* SOLDIERS.
Ay, steady now. Stand there. On guard.
BARTHOLOMEW (*Still looking toward the Left*).
They halt, consulting.—What? Can that be he?—
Velasquez, our sub-treasurer? Not so?
Juan de Travierra, too!
COLUMBUS. How strange!
Why, they were friends—and yet——
BARTHOLOMEW. They've left the rest—
Are coming here.
COLUMBUS. Alone?
BARTHOLOMEW. I think so.
COLUMBUS. Yes.
I recognize them now. You're right. 'Tis they.
I can't conceive, though, what it means. Can you?
BARTHOLOMEW. Who could?—The others have
begun to follow.
COLUMBUS. Aha! They think that these will seem
our friends:
And make an opening through which all can
enter.
What keener point could treachery find to edge
Its wedge of enmity, than tried old friendship?
(*To the* GUARD.)
Make ready.—Wait.

*Enter—Left Side Rear—*VELASQUEZ *and another officer. They bow and* COLUMBUS *addresses them.*

Well, what's your business here?

VELASQUEZ. We have been sent——

COLUMBUS.   True men are never sent
By their inferior. They will face him down;
And not turn tail like driven beasts of burden.

VELASQUEZ. You do not know our message.

COLUMBUS.   One may judge
A message from its messengers. I see
A crowd of common criminals. Were they
Set free by you, yourselves are criminals.

VELASQUEZ. Your pardon: but——

COLUMBUS. You should have asked for that
Before you freed your pals there. No one here
Has any right to pardon men but me.

VELASQUEZ. But you mistake——

COLUMBUS.   I am the Viceroy.
Traitors to him are traitors to the king.

VELASQUEZ. You may not be this now.

COLUMBUS.   What mean you?

VELASQUEZ (*handing him an official paper of which
he holds many*). Here,
'Tis from the court.

COLUMBUS (*taking and reading it*).
                          An outrage! Yet but gives
This Bobadilla—who? and what is he?—
Authority to make investigations.

Insulting !—Yet there's here no grant
For freeing captives that have been condemned.

VELASQUEZ (*handing* COLUMBUS *another roll*).
But here's another paper.

COLUMBUS (*receiving and reading it*).
                              That I yield
All prisoners, ships and royal property—
Why yes, if the investigation warrants —
Of course 'twill not.

VELASQUEZ.   Ah, but he says it does.

COLUMBUS.   It does?   Why, I have never seen this
          man.

VELASQUEZ.   Yet he's investigated. ——

COLUMBUS.   What ?

VELASQUEZ.   Your papers.

COLUMBUS.   My papers ? —Which and where ?

VELASQUEZ.   Those in your house.

COLUMBUS.   He's entered that ?

VELASQUEZ.   He lives there.

COLUMBUS.   In my house ?—
And reads my private papers?

VELASQUEZ.   They were found,
While carrying out his other orders.

COLUMBUS.   More ?

VELASQUEZ (*handing other papers to* COLUMBUS).
Yes, these.

COLUMBUS (*receiving and reading them*).
                    That I should pay all wages due
With all arrears for royal services —
What then ?

VELASQUEZ. He takes them from your property.

COLUMBUS. Without a word to me?—Why this
means ruin!
  And who decides the claims?—a man without
The means or inclination, as it seems,
To know the truth?—whose first official act
Is making friends by setting traitors free?
And violating both the laws of Spain
And common courtesy?—It is too much.
Away, and tell him I defy him. Say,
With all the rabble that are back of him,
Enough are here yet that are loyal still
To Spain and me, to crush one traitor more.

VELASQUEZ. I fear the loyal must be on his side.
    (Handing COLUMBUS *another paper.)*
Read this:--a royal patent that invests
This Bobadilla with all power and right
Of governing these islands.

COLUMBUS *(looking at the paper).*
                Royal seals?
  It cannot be—but yet--
    (Handing the paper to BARTHOLEMEW.)
                  Can it be true?
I knew that we had enemies; but not
That they could be so powerful.

BARTHOLEMEW.   We'll resist.

COLUMBUS. It might be useless; and it must be
wise
  To keep the right, when with us, with us still.

No no; we'll yield.   My brother, there are times
When wrongs are great that they may be per-
      ceived,
And emphasize the need of their redress.
      (*Turning to* GUTIERREZ *and the* GUARD.)
My men, this royal patent takes from me
The government: bestows what powers were
      mine
On Bobadilla.   All the loyalty
You've shown to me, for which my gratitude
Will always thank you, now belongs to him.
GUTIERREZ.   No, never.
GUARD.   Never.
Enter—Left Side—SANCHEZ, SOLDIERS, ESCOBAR,
      GAMEZ *and a rabble.*
      Enter—Right Side—PINTOR.
COLUMBUS.   'Tis the sovereign's will.
Help me by sharing with me what I bear.
            (*to* VALASQUEZ.)
Inform the governor we await his wishes.
VELASQUEZ.   There is another order.
COLUMBUS.   Eh?
VELASQUEZ.   It's with
      This officer.
            (*Gesturing toward* SANCHEZ.)
SANCHEZ (*advancing toward* COLUMBUS).
                        My orders—not desire.
COLUMBUS.   Am I to die for serving Spain so
      well?

SANCHEZ (*to both* COLUMBUS *and* BARTHOLEMEW).
  Not that—Your swords.

COLUMBUS (*as he and* BARTHOLEMEW *give up their
      swords, as does also* GUTIERREZ).
            But worse than that!—What next?

SANCHEZ (*motioning to a* SOLDIER *who brings for-
      ward some handcuffs.*)
  I act but for the court.

COLUMBUS.   Are those for me?
  What crime have I committed?

SANCHEZ.   I know none.

COLUMBUS.   I said I would submit.   You doubt my
    word?
  Or courage?—or persistency? or what?

SANCHEZ.   You're to be sent to Spain.

COLUMBUS.   In chains?—Who dares
  To place them on me?
      (*Looking at* SANCHEZ *and his* GUARD.)

SANCHEZ (*hesitating and looking around*).
            There's a large reward
  For him that does it.   Now 'tis offered.—Speak.
        (*to* COLUMBUS.)
  You see we're all your friends.

PINTOR.   Not all; not all!
      (*taking the handcuffs.*)
  Here, let me have them, boys. I'm used to
    them.
  A fair man gives what he receives, not so?
      (*Puts them on* COLUMBUS.)

Here, curse you !   Now fall overboard, and these
Will sink you, as we meant to, years ago.
(*Turning to* BARTHOLEMEW *and fastening another
pair on him.*)
Now you too.
RABBLE.   Ho, ho, ho !
COLUMBUS (*to* BARTHOLEMEW).

Bartholemew,
A single bracelet is enough, men think,
To show a common gratitude. · We've two.
They think their debt is doubled. How 'twill
    thrill
Ambition in the future sons of Spain
To learn what badges of true servitude
Await the souls that serve her best. We, we,
Who've made of Spain the Empress of the West,
Have weightier honors waiting us,—to be
The slaves that, crushed to earth, will pedestal
The towering contrast of her sovereignty.
*Exeunt—Left Side Front—*SANCHEZ, *his* SOLDIERS,
    COLUMBUS *and* BARTHOLEMEW.
    *Exeunt—to Left and Right—*OMNES.

———

SCENE SECOND—*A court belonging to a house in
Seville. Backing, and at the Right, parts of the
building on either side of the court. The same
at the Left, but near the Left Front entrance a*

*chair or two and a sofa with one end raised on
which to rest the head.*

Entrances—at Right Side—and Left Side.

(*Enter—Right Side—*DIEGO *and* BEATRIX.)

DIEGO.   You must not talk about his poverty.

BEATRIX.   Why not?

DIEGO.   You're killing him.

BEATRIX.   I'm nursing him.

DIEGO.   Yes, all that grows toward death.

BEATRIX.   If he had been
Content to leave the land to others, when
'Twas found once—

DIEGO.   Can a mother leave her child,
When born—no more?   'Twas less the land he
          sought,
Than those grand hopes his soul had based on it
As a foundation.

BEATRIX.   These he might have watched
As well at home here.

DIEGO.   Why, I thought 'twas you
That urged his seeking wealth.   The wealth was
          there,
And how about those titles?   All of them
Were labels not of use unless he sailed.

BEATRIX.   Why did he use them arbitrarily?

DIEGO.   Less use than their possession gave offense.
Besides, we men are trained to government
As much as manners.   'Tis the curse of force

That always its own method keeps alive
Its first excuse for being. Tyranny
May make of chaos order : but, when throned.
Knows not a subject that is not a slave.
Would one of those o'er whom my brother ruled,
Have bent the knee to an authority
Not ermined in the old familiar guise
Of arbitrariness ?

BEATRIX.   Had he conceived
How all would end !

DIEGO.   'Twas not conceivable.

BEATRIX. But you conceived it.

DIEGO.   I ?

BEATRIX.   Why yes. You spake
Of envy sure to follow.

DIEGO.   Did I so ?——

BEATRIX. And it came true.——'Tis often so with
      you—
Not that I like you better for it, though.

DIEGO. My words come true. eh ?—One might think
      they did ;
They are believed so seldom. 'Tis one test
Of prophets that they prophesy in vain.

BEATRIX. You might have urged your brother——

DIEGO.   Oh, not I !
I never urge myself.

BEATRIX.   But when you know—

DIEGO. Imagine only—not the same as knowing !
Imagination dreams, its dreams anon

May leap Time's processes, or keen-eyed, spy
The end from the beginning.   Yet such dreams
Come but to him so much in sympathy
With nature's courses, so inspired to aim
For nature's goals, so fired by nature's force,
That sheer inertia of the soul outspeeds
The pace of grosser matter.

BEATRIX.   And to you
    At times— —

DIEGO.   The times come seldom.   'Tis not oft
That fancy's flowers foretoken fruit : not oft
That fruit is laden on the limbs that bloom
Most brilliant with the flowers.—I've seen it
        though,—
Imagination imaging true life,
Life true to all its images : and then
I found a seer, earth's rarest product.

BEATRIX.   That
    Is what some say that you are.

DIEGO.   To be true
To life, when all the men that have life doubt me,
I ought to join with them, and doubt myself.

BEATRIX.   In that you're little like your brother.

DIEGO.   Ah,
With him quick action follows on the thought.
With me come only talk, and then more thought.
He mounts to find success.   I prophesy
Perhaps ; but where success is, at my best,
Am only of the crowds that cheer it.

(Looking to the Left.)

                                    Here
He comes, poor man—his faithful sons too. How
I love them for their faithfulness! Alas,
He's failing fast. If there was once a time
We feared he might be wrecked, he's reached a
    time
When wreckage has begun—with waves, too,
    worse
Than waves without, as much as stabs than
    scratches.
Fierce envy's made such havoc of his life,
'Twould not be strange if nature, in revolt,
Should doff the guise this world has torn to rags
And give him something richer.

> *Enter—Left Side—*COLUMBUS, *attended by his*
> *two sons,* YOUNG DIEGO, *a man, and*
> FERNANDO, *a youth.* COLUMBUS *with*
> *help is seated on the sofa.* DIEGO *continues*
> *to* COLUMBUS.

                              Well, what news?
COLUMBUS.   A new world has been found of bound-
    less wealth :
And he who found it, finds himself a beggar.
A king and queen were throned in that new world.
Who throned them there, they seized and bound
    in chains.
DIEGO.   Oh, yes ; but then the chains were taken
    off.

COLUMBUS. A nation has been made the first on
   earth.
  Who made it this, for this deed has been made
  The last in all that nation—not one shred
  Of all his property, or power, or rank,
  Stripped by injustice from him, when 'twas found
  To be injustice, has been given back.
  His name is left dishonored, and his sons
  Inherit nakedness.
BEATRIX.   Yes, that is it.
  You see if he——
DIEGO (*gesturing violently to silence* BEATRIX).
          Not now. The time will come——
BEATRIX (*suddenly turning her back upon* DIEGO *and
    speaking to herself*).
  Oh, when he prophesies, I always fear
  He's going to prophesy some ill of me.
        *Exit—Left Side—*BEATRIX.
DIEGO (*to* COLUMBUS).
  There's nothing that can dim your well-earned
   fame.
COLUMBUS. A man who gave his life for what to all
  Appeared impossible, attained it, then
  Found charts and notes that told his story, stolen,
  And that which was his own discovery,
  Called not by his own name but by another's.
DIEGO. Yes, it is very strange.
COLUMBUS.   So very strange
  It seems that when I think it can be true,
  11

I pause to listen to the morning bells
To wake me from a dream.

DIEGO.   'Tis but a dream.
The force that keeps eternal worth from light
Is but of time—a thing short-lived.

COLUMBUS.   I know—
If 'twere not for my children.——

YOUNG DIEGO.   They are proud
Of one who, all his life, as now in age,
Has stood alone, yet been victorious.

COLUMBUS.   Alone, and yet not lonely.   When one's
    true
To his own mission, he is in the ranks
With all that move toward all good ends that wait.
            (*Looking at his sons.*)
And but for you—think you I've lived my life
To beg men for a badge to brag about?—
Enough, if I have been an influence.

DIEGO.   Ay, that is all that God is.

COLUMBUS.   God?

DIEGO.   'Tis true.
What voice, or face, or form, or robe, or crown,
Or throne attests His Presence?   Who can trust
In things like these—what spirit serve but them,
And not be all through life—ay, out of it
And even after death—a slave to sense,
No brother of the Christ, no son of God?

(COLUMBUS *is seized by a sudden paroxysm and falls
        back upon the sofa.*)

FERNANDO. Why, see! He's fainting!

YOUNG DIEGO.   Help him!

DIEGO.   Ah? What's that?

    Why, Christopher!

    (*To the sons as all three bend over* COLUMBUS.)

                  Go, call a doctor—priest!

    Exeunt—Left Side Front—the two sons.)

COLUMBUS (*reviving and pointing toward the center of stage*).

The new world—you must watch it—it will grow.

Hark—there are words I hear—and look—FELIPA!

    (COLUMBUS *sinks in death supported by* DIEGO,

       who does not seem to notice what follows,

       being wholly absorbed in attending to

       COLUMBUS.)

SCENE THIRD:—*The curtain forming the back of Scene Second rises disclosing at the Left the same convent chapel and wall that occupy that place in Act First, Scene First. The convent wall, however, extends across the stage to the Right, and the whole Scene is backed by a distant view of a fertile, cultivated, and populous country, including mountains and valleys, rivers spanned by bridges, and low lands filled with towns and cities,—all representing the present condition of the western continent. Near the entrance of the chapel, stands* FELIPA, *gazing*

*toward this land, while, by a choir unseen within
the chapel, the same hymn is chanted as that with
which the drama opens, as follows :*

O, Life divine, thou art the spring
  Of all that germs and grows ;
The Light behind the suns that bring
  The harvests to their close.

O, Life divine, thou art the source,
  Of truth within the soul ;
Thou art the guide through all the course
  That leads it to its goal.

O, Life divine, what soul succeeds
  In aught on earth but he
Who moves as all desires and deeds
  Are lured and led by thee.

CURTAIN.

END.

BOOKS

From the Press of the Arena Publishing Company.

Is This Your Son, My Lord?

By HELEN H. GARDENER. The most powerful novel written by an American. A terrible *expose* of conventional immorality and hypocrisy. Price: paper, 50 cents; cloth, $1.00.

Pray You, Sir, Whose Daughter?

By HELEN H. GARDENER. A brilliant novel of to-day, dealing with social purity and the "age of consent" laws. Price: paper, 50 cents; cloth, $1.00.

A Spoil of Office.

A novel. By HAMLIN GARLAND. The truest picture of Western life that has appeared in American fiction. Price: paper, 50 cents; cloth, $1.00.

Lessons Learned from Other Lives.

By B. O. FLOWER.

There are fourteen biographies in this volume, dealing with the lives of Seneca and Epictetus, the great Roman philosophers; Joan of Arc, the warrior maid; Henry Clay, the statesman; Edwin Booth and Joseph Jefferson, the actors; John Howard Payne, William Cullen Bryant, Edgar Allan Poe, Alice and Phœbe Cary, and John G. Whittier, the poets; Alfred Russell Wallace, the scientist; Victor Hugo, the many-sided man of genius.

"The book sparkles with literary jewels." — *Christian Leader*, Cincinnati, Ohio.

Price: paper, 50 cents; cloth. $1.00.

For sale by all booksellers. Sent postpaid upon receipt of the price.

Arena Publishing Company,

Copley Square, BOSTON, MASS.

BOOKS

From the Press of the Arena Publishing Company.

The Dream Child.
A fascinating romance of two worlds. By FLORENCE HUNT-
LEY. Price: paper, 50 cents; cloth, $1.00.

A Mute Confessor.
The romance of a Southern town. By WILL N. HARBEN,
author of "White Marie," "Almost Persuaded," etc. Price:
paper, 50 cents; cloth, $1.00.

Redbank; Life on a Southern Plantation.
By M. L. COWLES. A typical Southern story by a Southern
woman. Price: paper, 00; cloth, $1.00.

Psychics. Facts and Theories.
By Rev. MINOT J. SAVAGE. A thoughtful discussion of
Psychical problems. Price: paper, 50 cents; cloth, $1.00.

Civilization's Inferno: Studies in the Social Cellar.
By B. O. FLOWER. I. Introductory chapter. II. Society's
Exiles. III. Two Hours in the Social Cellar. IV. The
Democracy of Darkness. V. Why the Ishmaelites Multiply.
VI. The Froth and the Dregs. VII. A Pilgrimage and a
Vision. VIII. Some Facts and a Question. IX. What of the
Morrow? Price: paper, 50 cents; cloth, $1.00.

---

*For sale by all booksellers. Sent postpaid upon receipt of
the price.*

Arena Publishing Company,

Copley Square,   **BOSTON, MASS.**

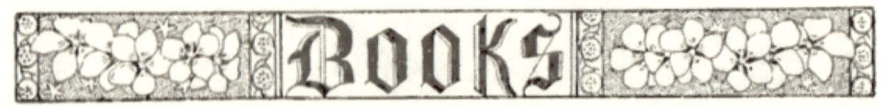

www.ingramcontent.com/pod-product-compliance
Lightning Source LLC
Chambersburg PA
CBHW030900050726
47500CB00009B/405